Other Books

by

Laura Federmeyer

Loren's Journey of Faith (2013)

Mystery of the Old Mill (2015)

Faith Continues Its Journey

Faith Continues Its Journey by Laura E. Federmeyer

Copyright © 2016 by Laura E. Federmeyer

Faith Continues Its Journey by Laura E. Federmeyer

Front Cover Picture by YANC at Canstock Photos

146p. ill. cm.

ISBN 978-1-935795-08-7

LCCN 2016913340

MRK Publishing

PO Box 353431

Palm Coast, FL 32135-3431

All characters and situations are fictional.

Dedication

This book is dedicated to all my friends and loved ones who enjoyed my first book, Loren's Journey of Faith and wanted to know what Loren and Andy did later.

Table of Contents

Prologue 1
Chapter One 3
Chapter Two 11
Chapter Three 25
Chapter Four 31
Chapter Five 41
Chapter Six 52
Chapter Seven 59
Chapter Eight 69
Chapter Nine 77
Chapter Ten 88
Chapter Eleven 98
Chapter Twelve 105
Chapter Thirteen 118
Chapter Fourteen 129
Epilogue 133
About the Author 136

FAITH CONTINUES ITS JOURNEY

BY:

LAURA E. FEDERMEYER

PROLOGUE

SEQUEL TO: LOREN'S JOURNEY OF FAITH

Jeremy ran his hand lightly over the hood of his new Italian sports car. After being polished, its silver color shone . He opened the door and slid behind the wheel. The doe-colored leather seats were smooth and soft to the touch. Jeremy looked at the instrument panel around the steering wheel. He smiled a crooked grin. It reminded him of his small airplane with all the gauges. If this car didn't pick up 'chicks' he didn't know what else to try. Ever since he had lost Loren Grayson to another man, he had not found another woman equal to her. She had been a challenge to his male ego in her 'ice princess' ways. Her dating standards were high. Loren would not let just anyone hold her hand. Touching her without permission was forbidden. Jeremy hadn't even been able to kiss her on the cheek or the mouth. Soon, though, Jeremy sought to solve that situation.

The motor purred as Jeremy put the car in gear. He leaned back against the soft leather seat. Maybe someday he would drive down to Waverly and find Loren. Surely by now she was bored with married life and would enjoy a day out with an old friend. Glancing in the rear view mirror Jeremy backed the car out of his driveway. Looking at his Rolex, he noted he had time to drive there and check out the town before he looked Loren up. From what he had heard, it was a hick town to be sure. This was going to be fun.

CHAPTER 1

Smoke began getting black and heavy as Loren tried to cover the burning skillet. Sally was there, holding the lid for Loren to place on the burning skillet. Sally tried to keep a straight face. Loren was going to be a challenge for her. The smoke alarm went off causing Andy to come running from the barn. He stopped short at the kitchen door grabbing the door frame to keep him from charging into the room.   The scene before him was almost laughable. Smoke was thick over the stove as it swirled about the kitchen. The stove vent was now working and the exhaust fan was sucking up the smoke.

Andy could see Loren's red face caused from the heat in the kitchen.   She was not a quitter. She would keep trying until she got it right.

Loren's first day in her 'cooking class' looked like a disaster.   He noted that Sally had everything partly under control so he slowly backed out of the room. Sally remained calm as she carried the hot skillet out onto the back porch to cool off.

"That's okay, Loren, honey. This is your first time. You will get better. Let's try something a little simpler."

Loren began again. Sally went slower with her directions as Loren tried to concentrate on each of the steps in putting a meal together. Soon, pleasant aromas were wafting through the kitchen.

Andy stood outside the door as he listened to Sally talk to Loren. How patient she was! Smiling to himself, he returned to the barn satisfied that he had made the right decision. Sally had jumped at the chance to come to the country for a visit on her vacation time from the Grayson household. She had just finished training a woman to take her place while she was on vacation. It was truly an answer to prayer! Andy no longer had to prepare the meals for the two of them. His dinner choices were getting old. Eating canned tuna and macaroni and cheese every other day was getting well, yuck! Loren would be able to cook on her own without burning everything. She did, however, learn how to boil water without burning it soon after they were married.

Loren closed the oven door on the casserole she had put in there. She set the timer and moved on to the next project. Sally had flour in a bowl and a rolling pin sitting beside it. Now, she would learn how to make biscuits.

"Sally, this is so much fun. I hadn't really known it could be this easy once you learned how to do everything. I'll try to pay attention and learn fast. Don't want you to start getting grey hairs and pull them out in frustration."

Sally laughed. "No worries about that, dearie. When I was at your parent's home, a couple cook's helpers learned under my instruction. They are now working in some of the largest restaurants in the city. We will prevail!" She clasped a hand on Loren's shoulder and grinned. The white marks of the flour left a handprint on her shoulder.

"Now, get your hands into this bowl of flour. I want you to get the feel of what you are working with. Here is the shortening to mix into the flour."

Loren stood over the bowl of flour at her kitchen counter. A frown of deep concentration was on her forehead as she dipped her hands into the flour mixture to stir in the shortening. A streak of flour was across Loren's face where she had swiped at a stray hair to get it back behind her ear. Sally had told her the feel of the batter was the trick to successful biscuits. Sally stood back a ways to watch without causing Loren to freak out. Her instructions were finally sinking in. This dinner should please everyone.

As Andy sat down to the delicious meal in front of him, he tried his best to eat slow and not appear too hungry. He could imagine his stomach jumping for joy at something edible coming its way. The burned meals and dried out food was now in the past.

Loren had learned how to cook a few decent items. Loren kept watching him, looking for signs of approval. Inwardly she grinned. She had done it! He liked it! Sally laid her fork down after cleaning off her plate. Her job was done. She had shown Loren the basics of cooking casseroles, pies, cookies and biscuits. A recipe file box sat on her counter containing other recipes for crock pot cooking, oven meat dishes, roasts, etc.

The whole process of teaching Loren how to cook only took three days. She had learned the secret of the recipes. A lot of prayer between the two of them had become necessary. They couldn't leave prayer out of the situation.

Andy and Loren stood on the front porch and watched the little compact car go on down their driveway. Sally raised her hand to wave farewell from the car as she drove away. What a trip!

Her patience had worn thin several times, but their understanding of each other along with the presence of Christ in their lives, they made it through. Now, thought Sally, I can go off for a couple of days to the beach and lay out in the sun. Sally chuckled, just thinking about spending time on the beach all by herself. What a change for someone like her a cook, who worked in a large household day in and day out. Time at the beach seemed a luxury for rich people, not the working class. Sally turned up the car radio and was soon caught up singing along with the song on the radio.

Loren had learned to successfully cook a couple decent

meals along with an easy recipe book to follow to make others. Andy was a meat and potato man with a short list of vegetables that he would eat. Basically all Loren had to do was not burn the meat. Her meatloaf was yet to be desired but it was passable. Her biscuits were so light, they almost needed to have something sitting on top of them to keep them from floating into the air. Her piecrusts were flakey like they are supposed to be. She had learned the difference between biscuit and pie dough. Biscuit mixture could stand being handled, but pie dough very little to stay light and flakey. Loren was on the way to becoming a good cook.

Now as they sat on the couch curled up together sipping on an iced tea, they opened their Bible to begin their evening devotions. With their radio playing softly in the background, Andy picked out the scripture for that evening.

***

Loren felt the rivet of sweat sliding down her back as she held the post that Andy was fastening the fencing wire to. One of the neighbor's cows had pushed it down trying to get to the rich green grass on their side of the fence. With the staples pounded into the post, Andy let go of the fence wire.

"There. We are finished. Let's hope Joe's cow stays home next time. Loren, can you grab the posthole digger and carry it up to the barn? I've got the rest of the tools."

Loren took the back of her hand and wiped the sweat off her

forehead. She hadn't planned on working so hard after they had gotten married. When she had worked in her father's shop, it had come easy even though the days were long. Putting electronic pieces into a hand-held phone was child's play next to farm work. Even though she sometimes longed for the easy life before marriage, she wouldn't even dream of going back. Andy was 'growing' on her. Every day as their love grew, they discovered new tidbits of each other's life. Little habits that had laid hidden came out occasionally. She had read somewhere that the first year of marriage was the testing and getting acquainted time.

With both of his hands, he pulled his sweat-soaked shirt off his back. He glanced over his shoulder watching Loren start to drag her feet. She was tired. Andy wiped his face with his wet shirt. They had gotten a lot done today.

Now Loren followed Andy into the barn to put away their tools. She almost didn't want to ask, 'what's next?'. Glancing at her wristwatch, she noted it was almost lunchtime. A break! Yea!

"Andy, how about some hamburgers on the grill for lunch?"

"Sounds good, Loren. Open up a can of beans to go with them. I think there is a bag of potato chips in the pantry. I'll get the tools put away and be up shortly to start the grill."

Andy went off in another direction toward the barn and tool shed while Loren headed for the house. When he closed the front door behind him, he heard the shower running. Loren was taking her shower. He went into the kitchen and got out everything he needed to fix their lunch. In the pantry, he found the potato chips and can of pork and beans. There was a new batch of chocolate chip cookies in the cookie jar and a fresh pitcher of brewed iced tea in the refrigerator. When Loren came into the kitchen, she started preparing the meal where Andy had left off.

With the meal finished, Andy sat in the living room with his legs stretched out on the coffee table. Loren came in from the kitchen carrying a couple glasses of iced tea and cookies. Andy smiled, remembering Loren's first attempt at baking cookies. She had gotten a recipe for peanut butter cookies. She followed the directions, placing the round balls of dough on the cookie sheet. Into the oven they went with the thoughts that they would flatten out as they baked. The directions were not complete. Each cookie was supposed to be pressed down with a fork to make them flat. Andy chuckled. He had taken the 'peanut butter cookies' outside and used them as balls to hit with his golf club. Loren tilted her head sideways as she watched Andy trying to hold back his chuckle.

"What's so funny?"

"I was remembering the time you made those peanut butter cookies. Remember? I used them for practice with the golf club. They really went a long way. I should have given them to your dad to use for his golf game."

"Ha Ha. Very funny. It was the person who submitted that

recipe to the cookbook maker. How was anyone to know they were supposed to be flattened before cooking? From now on, I am making chocolate chips. Sally went through the whole process and I have successfully made a batch. You are eating them now. You thought they are Sally's, but no, they are mine! Any last words before you die of cookie poison?"

Both of them laughed together.

CHAPTER 2

Breathing heavily after a hard run, eight year old Kit bent over behind a large bush and fell to his knees. He twisted around so he could look out toward the road. Through the branches, he watched the long black car driving slowly past. He waited until the car was down the road and out of sight before he stood up, still leaning over to keep hidden.   The sun had not set as yet so he could easily be seen through the bushes. His reddish brown hair was wet with perspiration and sticking out all over his head. He had run fast a long way and his sides hurt .   Kit ran a sleeve across his forehead to wipe the sweat from it. Still down on his knees, he tightened both of his tennis shoe laces. His right knee that he had scraped on the pavement while jumping out of the car began to hurt. Now looking around, he tried to figure out where he was and where to go next. The orphanage cops would soon double back and research the area where he had jumped out of the car to make his get-away. He had to move and fast.

A dirt driveway seemed to beckon him a short distance away. Slowly he made his way in that direction and walked quickly down it toward the farmhouse he could see back behind the tree line. Every so often, he stopped to glance back toward the main road. The coast was clear. So far no one was following him. He didn't want to go to a third foster home. When his parents had abandoned him at the orphanage three years ago, he was determined to escape and find a good home.

The foster homes he had been in, the parents had argued almost constantly and was abusive to him and the other children under their care.   Kit was only eight, but felt he could survive on his own for awhile until he found his 'perfect' place.

The whinny of a horse caused him to perk up his ears. A horse! If there was one thing he could say he really loved, it would be a horse. Although he had never been around any or even touched one, he loved them. Just knowing a horse was nearby pleased him to no end. Maybe he could fulfill one of his childhood dreams of riding one. His steps were quicker now as he neared the farm yard. Stopping short of crossing the large open area, he looked for any kind of movement. Seeing no one or hearing a dog barking, he raced across the yard. He came to a stop beside the high corral fence holding the horse. The horse was prancing and snorting at the intruder to scare him away.

Ranger snorted again, then charged the fence. Kit looked

through the rails at the big reddish brown horse that had now come to a stand-still looking at the boy. Being scared more than curious, Kit stood still. Ranger slowly ventured over toward the boy. He snorted and shook his head. The boy held his position. He didn't seem to pose a threat. Ranger was not about to get any closer. Even though Ranger was used to 'little' people, this boy did not look dangerous. The boy was not holding a carrot or an apple. He was an intruder! Ranger snorted again, tossing his head.

The back door of the barn opened fairly easily as Kit walked around the corral to the barn door and slipped inside. He searched some of the food bins and found some apples. He took two and walked over to the stairs leading to the loft.

Up there, he could maybe stay for awhile. The hay was prickly to lay down on. It would have to do until he could find blankets to use. He sat cross-legged on a bale of hay eating one of the apples. Maybe after dark he could sneak up to the house and get in to find food in the refrigerator.

He watched through the slats in the loft floor as Andy and Loren milked the cow and fed the livestock. They looked like a nice couple. Would they accept him if he was caught? As the sun took its journey down behind the trees, darkness fell. Kit climbed down the ladder before it got too dark to see where he was going and looked out across the yard. No one stirred. He waited for the lights in the house to go out before creeping up closer to the house. No dogs. Great! Silence, then Kit heard them reading something. Andy and

Loren were having their evening devotions.

"In the beginning was the Word and the Word was with God, and the Word was God. The same was in the beginning with God. All things were made by him, and without him was not any thing that was made. In him was life, and the life was the light of men. And the light shineth in darkness and the darkness comprehended it not."

Kit listened through the partly open window near the back door. He wrinkled up his nose. It sounded like scripture. It wasn't Sunday! Did people actually read from the Bible on weekdays?

His eyes became as round as saucers as he watched them holding hands and bowing their heads. Each one took turns praying. As they both said Amen, Andy stood up taking Loren's hand pulling her to her feet. It had been a long day for both of them.

They were ready to 'hit the hay'. Kit watched them leave the room and go toward the back of the house. Soon, the lights were out and all was dark and silent. Kit waited a good half hour before going to the back door.

Putting a hand on the knob, he turned slowly. It was unlocked. Holding his breath against a squeaking door, he eased the door open. He slipped inside and closed the door. Standing still until his eyes became accustomed to the darkness in the house, he slowly breathed easier. Now, as he stood in front of the refrigerator, he opened the door. Wow! So much food to have! His mouth watered. It had been a long time since he had eaten anything.

All the food he could really devour was there and it all didn't require cooking. He quickly made his choices and moved on into the pantry. Several flip-top cans offered more meals and fruit for dessert. Kit found a plastic grocery bag near-by and filled it with the things he had picked out. He just took what he would eat that night and in the morning. He could probably go back to the house later that day if the couple ventured somewhere in the car. Plastic silverware was grabbed along with plates and napkins. Plastic cups and bottled water were there to grab, too. He found a couple large towels near the back door he could use to make his bed. Quickly he moved back out of the back door, closing it quietly.

Back in the loft, he carefully placed his food on the floor beside a bale of hay. Tomorrow, he would try to find a couple of blankets and maybe a pillow.

Right now, he ate and then made up a bed. Morning would come soon and there would be activity in the barn again when the man came out to feed the animals and milk the cow he had seen in a back stall.

The next day, Kit watched the two get into a jeep and drive away after the barn chores were finished. He was free to roam about the property. Now would be a good time to return to the house and seek out a couple of blankets. Scratching his back against the barn door, he wiggled about trying to get comfortable after sleeping on the hay. As he walked around the back of the barn, Ranger charged the fence snorting, scaring Kit. The intruder was still there! Kit slowly approached the fence. By talking to the horse in low soothing tones he hoped to get the horse in a more friendly mood.. Ranger perked up his ears and listened. This boy might sound nice, but that didn't hide the fact that he was not supposed to be there.

Kit had soon started telling the horse all his problems, what he wanted in life and where he wished he could be. As a few tears escaped down his cheek, he swiped at them with his shirt sleeve. He knew the horse would not understand a word that he said, but just talking out loud made him feel better.

As the day passed on toward lunchtime, Kit brought out an apple from the feed bin. He had found an old steak knife that he used to slice up the apple. Going back to the corral fence, he called to Ranger.

"How about me sharing this apple with you. I'm sure that you like them or they wouldn't be in your feed bin. Come on, boy, let's be friends."

Ranger snorted at Kit. He charged the fence causing Kit to jump back. He stumbled backwards and fell to the ground. Ranger horse laughed at him, tossing his head in victory. Kit scrambled to his feet, dusting off his pants.

"Okay, you win this round. I only want to be friends and maybe scratch your ears."

Ranger's ears perked up. That was a word he understood! An ear scratching really would feel good about now. Could he trust this little person? He had not had much contact with small people since he had lived at the stables giving riding lessons to kids. He cocked his head sideways and looked at this kid in front of him.   If he could be scared just charging the fence, then Ranger felt that he could control the touching of this small person. Slowly Ranger backed away from the fence. Kit came over to the fence, then slipped through the bars to stand near Ranger. He didn't move. He would let the horse make the first move.

Ranger took a couple steps toward the boy, then lowered his head and thrust out his nose. Breathing in the smell of the boy, he felt no reason to back off or to scare the boy again. Kit reached out a hand and touched Ranger's soft muzzle with the tips of his fingers. Slowly he worked his fingers up onto Ranger's forehead, sort of scratching as he went. The horse's ears were up. That was a good sign. Kit had read about watching for certain signals and now was still cautious. The horse could still turn on him and attack.

Ranger nibbled on Kit's hair, blowing his hot breath into his ear. It tickled. Kit chuckled. Leaving all caution behind, Kit threw his arms around Ranger's neck, hugging him. With his face against the horse's neck, Kit fought back the tears threatening to come out. Ranger started to pull away. They needed to get acquainted first. Kit didn't know how much longer he could secretly stay there in the barn. He desired a bath and a good meal. He didn't dare try to do that in the house not knowing when the couple would return.

Ranger bumped Kit with his nose to remind him that he was still waiting for that ear scratch the boy had mentioned.

Kit found immense pleasure in scratching the inside of

Ranger's ears with his thumbs and around the back of them. Ranger's back itched also, but that was getting too familiar. The boy was a stranger. He didn't belong there. Besides, the boy couldn't even reach his back. He would have to stand on something and even then stretch on his toes.

Ranger's head came up, his ears pricked forward. A car was coming! Kit saw it and quickly scooted under the fence. When Ranger turned his head back around, the boy was gone. Andy and Loren were home.

Loren began putting the groceries away. She noticed that some of their canned goods were missing. She hadn't restocked those items because she knew that she had some already. Some items in the refrigerator were missing also. They had been some leftovers they had planned to fix for dinner that night. Andy came in carrying the last bag from the car.

"What's wrong?"

"Some of our food is missing. I didn't buy certain items because I knew I already had them in the pantry. Even the piece of meat loaf I was going to have for dinner tonight is gone. Do you suppose someone broke in and stole some of our food?"

"There hasn't been any homeless people that I know of passing through. Ranger would have alerted us if someone came near the barn. Maybe I had better check out the barn just in case. I haven't been up in the loft for a couple of days. I'll go do that. Check around and see if anything else is missing."

"All right. Be careful."

Kit saw him coming. Oh, oh. He was about to be caught! He shouldn't have taken the meat loaf. It had been fairly good cut thick between two slices of bread. He hurried down the ladder to the loft, then slipped out the back door. As he reached the few bushes in the back, he thought about all his personal stuff in the loft. He might as well give up. Maybe they would be nice folks and let him stay awhile.

Andy had seen him go behind the bush when he came around the barn. He hadn't even gone in the barn to search the loft. He could just barely see Kit's reddish hair through the bushes. Red hair was hard to hide.

"All right, you can come out. We don't shoot strangers under five feet tall."

Kit almost laughed. Was this guy serious? Slowly he stood up and walked around the bush to stand before Andy. Instantly he liked Andy's looks.

He would deserve straight answers.

"So, you were brave enough to eat my wife's meatloaf. No belly aches? I guess it wasn't too bad because you are still alive. Now, who are you and where do you belong?"

"My name is Kit. I am running from an abusive foster home. I really like it here. Your horse is cool."

Ranger is my wife's horse. What did you do to get on his good side? He is supposed to be our 'watch horse' since we don't have a dog yet."

"I shared an apple with him when I first came here and today it was a good ear scratching."

Andy stroked his chin and tried to look serious. "How old are you?"

"Going on nine."

"Well, it looks like you would like to have a bath and clean clothes. We just bought some ice cream. Come on up to the house with me and we will talk some more."

"You won't call the authorities on me just yet? I have clean clothes up in the loft."

"You go get them. I'll wait for you right here."

"Yes, sir!" Kit took off back into the back door of the barn and up into the loft. He retrieved his backpack that had a change of clothes in it and came back down. Together they walked up to the house.

"Loren, we have our burglar. He is really a brave one. He ate your meatloaf."

Loren turned around and looked at the small boy standing beside Andy. She joined in with Andy's teasing. "He is still alive! What a wonderful miracle! Maybe my cooking is improving."

Kit looked first to Loren, then back at Andy. Was she for real?

"Loren, this is Kit. He needs a nice soak in the tub and he brought a change of clothes with him. How about showing him the bathroom and getting him started. I promised him ice cream when he is done."

"You are bribing a burglar? Goodness gracious. Come on, Kit. We'll get you cleaned up and then we can all have some ice cream."

Loren took Kit back to the bathroom and started the water to fill the tub. When Kit told her he would rather shower, she stopped the water. She showed him how the knobs worked, then gave him a big fluffy towel to use.

"Just come on out in the kitchen when you are done. Call if you need anything."

"Yes, Ma'am."

While Kit was in the shower, Loren made up the bed in the spare bedroom. The boy would not spend another night out in the barn loft. Having a boy around the farm seemed like a wonderful idea. He seemed well mannered and maybe he could be at home there. She was curious on how he had gotten past Ranger's watchfulness. The horse usually let them know if someone strange was on the property.

When she returned to the living room, Andy told her about catching Kit and how he had gotten past Ranger's defenses. They would have to get a dog sometime soon.

A watchdog would be a good thing to have out there in the country like they were. Kit came into the kitchen where they were sitting. A lock of his hair refused to be combed down and stuck up on the back of his head. He sat down and waited for either of them to speak. He was prepared to be sent back to the family he had fled from. He told himself, this has been just a short vacation. His freedom ended here. He had enjoyed the visit, now to face the music.

Loren placed a dish of ice cream in front of him and Andy opened the cookie jar filled with some of Sally's chocolate chips. Kit could almost taste the cookies before he was handed a couple. They still even felt warm! Some of the chocolate chips had melted and as he took his first bite, the chocolate oozed out like melted cheese.

Loren looked on with a smile on her face. He was showing the same expression that she had when she had taken the first bite of that wonderful cinnamon roll on her journey on horseback to Waverly. Oh, that had been a really wonderful experience! If Brownie , her packhorse, had not lost one of his shoes, she would not have met the blacksmith and his wife who made the most delicious cinnamon rolls.

On their horseback camping trip back from their wedding and stopping at the same campsites was really not the same as when she had done it on her own the first time. Andy had done all of the tent setting up and almost all the chores around the campsite. All she got to do was feed the horses and set out the table settings. The urge to do it all again on her own entered her thoughts.

It just might be fun to do it again without Andy. Maybe the

boy would like to come along. She glanced over at Andy and caught him looking at her with a questioning look on his face. Oh, oh. She had raised his curiosity. Now what? Her mind scrambled for something to say to divert his thoughts.

"Uh, Kit. Do you know how to ride a horse?"

"No, madam. I have only been across the fence from yours. He don't seem too friendly."

"Ranger is supposed to be our 'watch dog'. You have been here several days?"

Kit nodded. He grabbed up his napkin and wiped the cookie crumbs from his lips.

"He *did* let me know I was not welcome, though. Does that count? He couldn't chase me off the property, him being in the corral and all. I've only been here one night."

Andy stood up and took his ice cream dish out into the kitchen. Loren followed with her dish. After setting them in the sink, Andy looked at her.

"What are we going to do with him? I wouldn't mind having him around here for awhile to help out and give him some relief from what he seems to have been through. I'll call the authorities and find out what we need to do to make it happen. He seems like a nice kid and well mannered. Say, what was the idea behind asking him if he could ride a horse? We don't have a small horse."

"Could we get one of those ponies from Joe, next door? We could borrow it for awhile to see if Kit likes to ride. It has been awhile since we went riding together anyhow."

"Okay. I'll check with the authorities and see what they have to say and then we can go 'pony shopping'."

As it turned out, the authorities were more than willing to let Loren and Andy keep Kit. They had checked with the foster parents and they had had enough of Kit's antics and constantly running away. When the authorities did some further checking on the former foster family, they found several other youngsters still in their care not being cared for properly. In a few weeks someone from their department would come out and show them the paperwork to become Kit's new foster parents.

Kit was ecstatic. Already he felt at home. They did need to go back to the former foster family and secure all of his belongings. Andy drove him there to get his things.

The next day they would go next door and pick out a pony for him to ride.

CHAPTER 3

Joe had a couple of Welsh ponies along with a few Shetlands. As Kit was in the corral with all six of them, one of the Welsh ponies seemed to be the friendliest toward Kit. Its golden color with a fluffy white tail and long mane reminded him of peanut butter and whipped cream. The pony nudged him with his nose causing Kit to laugh. Joe and Andy watched. The pony was a perfect match. Joe came over and put a halter on the pony, then led it out of the corral. He tied it to a hitching post, then disappeared in the barn. He brought out a couple of brushes and tack. Kit was handed a brush and was given his first lesson on how to take care of the pony.

With the pony saddled and ready to ride, Kit attempted to get into the saddle. He finally pulled himself up and settled down in the saddle. The saddle stirrups were adjusted for Kit's feet. Andy walked beside him as they went back towards home. As he walked alongside Kit, he told him how to hold the reins, sit in the saddle and how to position his feet in the stirrups. Kit listened and paid attention. He felt like he was on top of the world! He had seen lots of westerns on TV and wondered if he would ever be able to ride a horse like that. He had met several boys and girls older than him at school who had horses and rode all the time. None offered to let him ride their horses, though.

Once they were home, Andy put Ranger in the back pasture and put Kit and the pony in the corral to practice riding. Ranger watched the two in 'his' corral.

The little fella now had his own horse. Would he still be willing to scratch his ears? With a snort, Ranger whirled around and crow-hopped along the fence line. When he saw no one was watching him, he put his head down and began to eat the grass under his feet.

Later that day, Loren caught Ranger and brought him in to be brushed and saddled. Ranger watched Andy go and get his horse to do the same. Anticipation grew as Ranger was anxious to venture out on the trails far beyond the back fence. Kit watched from atop his pony. They were all going for a ride! Wow!

"Okay, Kit. Let's go riding. You can show us what you learned today."

Together the three walked their horses off through the gate and on toward the back lot. Andy closed the gate behind him so the cow wouldn't decide to walk around in the front yard and eat all

Loren's flowers along the front walkway.

Ranger tossed his head as he pulled on the reins, wanting to go faster. Loren pulled back to let him know they were not going to run today. Kit was along and he needed to learn to ride better first. Loren tried to convey the message to Ranger through a few gentle pulls back on the reins. He finally got the message and turned his head to look at the boy riding the pony. Horses are not supposed to have reasoning capabilities, but Ranger seemed to. Horses also were not supposed to experience jealousy, but he did. Maybe it was just first time impressions. He let out a snort, then settled down to enjoy the outing.

Kit was getting a little tired of sitting in the saddle and bouncing. He was watching Andy and Loren ride and tried to imitate their posture. He noted the shorter legs of the pony in comparison to the longer strides of the larger horses. No wonder his pony was moving differently. He would have to develop his own riding rhythm. Just when he thought he had the feel down pat, they turned the horses around to go back.

"Do you feel like trying a faster pace, Kit?"

"Will it be smoother?"

"Don't know." chuckled Andy. "Let's give it a try. Just pull back on the reins if the pace is too fast and you lose your balance."

Andy touched his horse with his heels, sending it into a trot, then faster as they loped. Loren joined him. The pony began its attempt to keep up.

Kit grasped the saddle horn and hung on tightly. With the little bit of bouncing, he was excited. He was riding a running horse! The wind felt good on his face as his hair flew in all directions. He remembered the movie with John Wayne where he had charged the bad guys with the reins in his mouth and a smoking gun in each hand, firing as he rode. Even though he was tempted to try putting the reins in his mouth and wave both hands in the air, he thought better of it. This was his first day on a horse. He had a lot of learning and practicing to do.

The three soon slowed their horses and brought them back into a slow walk. Kit learned that running a horse back to the barn was a *very bad idea.* Back at the barn, everyone dismounted. Kit soon found out what saddle-sore was.

Stiffly he walked around some to get his 'land-legs' back . He put the halter back on the pony, then tied it to the corral fence. Andy showed him how to remove the saddle and where to store his gear in the tack room. He picked up a brush and comb, then returned to brush down the pony before putting it in the corral with Ranger. Ranger stuck his head over and sniffed the pony. The pony made a little squeal, jerking his head back. Kit lost his hold on the brush as the pony's head came back knocking it out of his hand. When Kit looked up at Ranger, he looked like he hadn't done anything. Kit laughed. He picked up the brush and started again where he had left off. Ranger was really an unusual horse.

With the horses put away and everything in its rightful place, the trio went back up to the house. Loren poured some lemonade into iced over glasses and they sat down in the living room. They didn't need for Kit to tell them how much he had enjoyed the ride. They could tell. Some rules would have to be made that would keep him safe in this new environment. A few were given to him right then. There were too many rules to give him all at once. He had only arrived and everything would soon become routine. It was time for showers.

While the clean-up process was going on, Loren moved into the kitchen to come up with a dinner plan. Hamburgers on the grill sounded yummy along with baked beans and French fries.

With the meal over and all the barn chores done, Kit was ready to fall asleep. A couple times they caught him almost falling asleep while eating.

They ushered him to his room and said good night. Returning to the living room, Andy and Loren began planning their church activity with the youth group. At least 15 teenagers were to converge on their home that Saturday. They had done the study of where the teenage hotspots were in town. All of them were 'city' kids, none knew about farm life. Some had grandparents who farmed, but the visits to their homes were very sparse. The teenagers were content to stay in town where lots of activities provided escape from being at home where sometimes parents bossed them around to help with the housework, etc. A few of them had heard about the new couple who were going to help at the church. Maybe their curiosity would send them over to check it out. With the whole summer coming, they would need different diversions to satisfy their boredom.

Somehow the ideas and plans for the teenagers would come together and everything would go smoothly. Through spying on the teens, they discovered where they spent most of their time when school was not in session or on the weekends, the movies, video arcade store, or just shopping at the local mall. The town had a well equipped park where all kinds of sports could be played. There was no bowling alley, but traveling to a nearby city could fulfill that activity.

CHAPTER 4

Andy followed Loren through the house picking up empty plates and cups. The church youth group had showed up in full force anxious to meet their new leaders.

After returning to Waverly from their honeymoon on horseback, Andy and Loren had started helping in the local church trying to build up a youth group. The church was small and very few families supported it. Children were nil. Everyone was either grandparent age or older. Nothing exciting within the church could draw any of the youth in Waverly. They were not interested in God.

Through many planning meetings with the pastor and staff, Andy and Loren began working on a plan. For the next couple of weeks, they sort of spied on the teenagers. They followed them to different places where they hung out to see what they enjoyed doing. Video games, movies and loud music seemed to attract the majority of them. Through some digging, Loren discovered some of the girls were interested in make-up, cooking, going shopping and general things a mother should be showing their daughters. Parents worked. There didn't seem to be a stay at home mother in today's world.

After finishing the clean-up process, Loren grabbed two glasses of iced tea in the kitchen and brought them into their family room. Andy uncrossed his legs and folded up the newspaper he had been reading. Loren was ready to talk. He had noticed her for the last hour acting like she was forming a speech in her head. He halfway grinned.

They hadn't been married very long and already he was beginning to be able to read her thoughts.

He watched her set down the iced tea glasses on the coffee table in front of them.

"Okay, have we any ideas on the girls?" asked Andy as he leaned over to pick up a glass. Loren turned toward him as she stuffed a couch pillow behind her. She smiled at him, then picked up her own glass before speaking.

"We need to plan some parties. The girls can meet here for a tea party. I'm going to ask Peggy at the beauty salon if she can help me with the girls' hair and maybe make-up. I'm not that familiar with all the different kinds of hair styles or kinds of make-up.. Peggy might know someone who would volunteer. How about the boys?"

Andy took another swallow of iced tea before setting the

glass down. "If I can talk to some of them, they might be interested in wood working. Joe, our next door neighbor, has some wood we could use to cut and make bird houses or something else simple to start. I haven't visited the high school to see if they have a shop class. The video arcade downtown seems to be the place where most of them hang out. I'm going to check and see if the owner would close one night and just be open to our boys. We can have maybe a pizza and Bible study along with games. I noticed that some of the boys did not make the varsity teams for their school sports. Maybe we can get them in some basketball games at the Park. They just might appreciate a chance to play where their grades don't have to count to stay on a team.

If we can't get the kids inside the church, we need to go where they are. The park next to the church has a full size basketball court where I could get the boys to play. Maybe some of the boys who didn't make the main varsity squad would like a chance to play."

"Well, we have some idea as to the direction we want to take. Now, we just need to get the wheels of progress to turn."

Kit peeked his head around the door. He had spent the last couple hours in his room trying out the new video game Andy had set up for him.

"Is it okay to come in? Party all over?"

"Yeah, for now. Were we too noisy?"

"Naw. Did you find out what those kids want? Sounds like

they are not interested in what you want them to learn."

Loren motioned Kit to come over and sit down with them. Maybe this boy who was at least four years younger could shed some light on this subject.

"We are trying to interest those teens into attending church."

"What kind of music do you have at your church?"

"Why it's the old traditional songs we have sung all our lives."

"This is a new generation. We don't want to hear all those old slow moving down-beat songs. What is that other kind of church music called?"

"Contemporary. It is mostly praise songs and sung like rock 'n roll."

"Have you ever been to one of those services? How do you know if those songs will work?"

Andy ruffled Kit's hair. "Just when did you become so smart?"

"I have a CD in my room. Let me play some of the music."

Before either could give him an answer, he had headed for his room. When he returned, Loren put the CD in the player.

The first song was the theme for the play, JESUS CHRIST, SUPER STAR. The song AS THE DEER PANTETH came next. OPEN MY EYES LORD

Several rock 'n roll sounding ones came next, but they could understand the words. It conveyed Jesus dying on the cross for all the sins of the world.

A song naming off the beatitudes came next. Kit even had a CD by the Newsboys with the song *I Believe.*

Andy and Loren were almost spellbound. They really hadn't heard much of any of those particular songs. Maybe Kit had something there. They could use them on a Sunday night service after they got some commitments from the teens to attend at least once.   As the song LIFT YOUR NAME ON HIGH played the last verse, Loren smiled at Andy. This *had* to be their solution! She scrambled through her papers for a blank sheet of paper. Here, she wrote the names of the songs down on it. As she wrote, out of the corner of her eye, she saw Andy 'high five' Kit.

"Now, young man. What do you know about video games?"

Kit laughed. This was going to be fun. He got to tell the 'older' people how things were with the teens and younger kids. As he talked, Loren took notes. She had to present the ideas to the pastor and staff before they could continue executing them.

Kit ventured out into the yard and headed for the barn. Ranger saw him coming and nickered a greeting. The cream colored pony moved alongside him and waited also.

He had heard from Ranger about the wonderful ear scratches the boy did and wanted one, too. Kit laughed at the two horses as they vied for his attention at the same time. He stood still waiting for each horse to stand on either side of him.

Now, he could reach both of them at the same time! The silly horses! He wondered how the pony knew about the ear scratching. Did the horses communicate with each other? They must.

After giving both a good ear scratching, Kit ventured on into the barn. He could start cleaning out a couple of stalls while he waited for Andy to come out to start milking the cow and feeding everyone.

***

Jeremy ran his hand lightly over the hood of his new Italian sports car. After being polished, its silver color shone . He opened the door and slid behind the wheel. The doe-colored leather seats were smooth and soft to the touch. Jeremy looked at the instrument panel around the steering wheel. He smiled a crooked grin. It reminded him of his small airplane with all the gauges. If this car didn't pick up 'chicks' he didn't know what else to try. Ever since he had lost Loren Grayson to another man, he had not found another woman equal to her. She had been a challenge to his male ego with her 'ice princess' ways. Her dating standards had been high or old fashioned as someone had told him.

Holding her hand or even trying to touch her was a no-no. Jeremy hadn't even been able to kiss her cheek let alone on the mouth.

The motor purred as Jeremy put the car in gear. He leaned back against the soft leather seat . Looking at his Rolex, he noted he had time to drive there and check out the town before he looked Loren up. From what he had heard, it was a hick town to be sure. This was going to be fun. Surely by now she was bored with married life and would enjoy a day out with an old friend. Glancing in the rear view mirror Jeremy backed the car out of his driveway.

Jeremy slowly toured Waverly. What a dump! True, the town was neat and clean, but nothing like the city. There was only one local bar where he stopped to get a beer.

Jeremy questioned some of the patrons, to learn where Loren and Andy Camden lived, but no one knew them. Those patrons did not attend church, so they knew nothing about Loren or Andy. As Jeremy was walking back to his car, he spotted Loren walking along the sidewalk heading for the Beauty Shop. He turned around in the middle of the street and quickly walked toward her.

"Hello, stranger." he greeted.

Loren stopped walking and stared at Jeremy. What was he doing there? Remembering her manners as a lady, she greeted him.

"Jeremy. What a pleasant surprise. What brings you out into the country?"

"I thought you would be bored and lonely for the city life, so I came to rescue you. Come and see my new car."

He almost took her arm, then realized she would still hold to her standards.

Dropping his arm, he waited. Loren looked across the street at the car. It was really sharp looking and looked fast. Its silver coat shone despite the dusty roads.

"It looks like it was made for you, Jeremy. I'll bet it is fast, too."

"Come on and take a ride. We'll go into the city and have a nice meal together. We can catch up on everything that has been going on since we saw each other."

Loren shook her head, remembering the first time she rode in a car with Jeremy.

He had spiked her drink making her appear drunk and tried to kidnap her. Andy had rescued her from the lake after Andy had run Jeremy's car off the road and it had slid down the bank into the water at the edge of the lake. A few more minutes longer would have seen the car slide into the water and possibly sink.

Now, Loren had to come up with some way out of this situation. She was almost positive that if she walked over to the car, Jeremy would try to force her into it. Making a quick glance around, there was no one on the walk or nearby who would come to her aid if she yelled 'help'. So far, Jeremy was being a gentleman. He had not touched her nor tried to. Slowly Loren stepped back out of his reach. Jeremy wondered if he would have another chance at her if he came back another time. He decided to gamble on it. He would wait. He let her back away knowing she was remembering that time at the party.

"Okay, Loren. You have won this round. I will maybe see you again sometime and you will be more receptive to my invitation. You have always been the woman for me, even though I have courted others. You know that I am a gentleman and will take good care of you. Our first time was a mistake. I had had too much to drink at the party. I hope you can forgive me for that."

His apology surprised Loren, but she was still pleased to receive it. Up until then, he had kept her at arms length and honored her wishes not to be touched. He said his good-bys and walked over to his car. With a little show of power, he whipped the car around on the street and took off with a squeal of tires.

Loren watched, inwardly shivering at her close call. She sat down on one of the iron benches along the walk to regain her composure. She lifted up a short prayer of thanks before standing up. Never in a million years did she expect Jeremy to show up like that in Waverly. Hopefully he had taken the hint to leave her alone. Their relationship, if he could call it that, was dead.

Now, she was ready to go into the beauty shop and tell the owner what she had in mind for the teenagers. The thoughts of Jeremy were soon forgotten.

The coolness of the air conditioner inside the beauty shop was like a breath of fresh air for Loren. The smell of the chemicals used for the permanents in hopes of making a person beautiful was strong, but did not hinder the coolness of the air conditioner. Several women were there getting something done to their hair. The weekend was coming and several activities in the town had been planned.

The women wanted to look their best. Peggy, the owner of the shop, came over toward Loren smiling.

"Hello, Loren. What can we do for you today?"

Loren smiled and took Peggy's offered hand. "We have been trying to get the teenagers into church. With summer coming on, they will need some activities to keep them occupied and out of trouble. Andy, the pastor and I have tried to come up with some ideas for the teens. What do you think of teaching the girls how to do their hair and apply make-up?"

"That would cut into my business if I gave out free help." Peggy paused. She had spoken too quickly. The teenagers didn't come into her shop anyhow. Maybe this would be a way of getting more customers. At least maybe a couple of their mothers. Their mothers might just see the changes in their daughters and venture in for a make-over for themselves.

"I spoke too soon, Loren. Maybe we could work out a plan. Do you have any ideas on how you want to work this?"

Loren shook her head. "When you have a free hour, let us get together and work out something. I don't even know if the girls around here would be interested. We might have to get at least two to be sort of guinea pigs. They could show their friends what they learned, then maybe, just maybe the rest will come."

"Sounds like a good plan to me. Let me check my schedule."

CHAPTER 5

Shelly sat in a chair near the window of the beauty shop awaiting her turn. Five girls had opted to go with Loren and learn how to style their hair. One of her long dark brown locks hung over her left shoulder and she was nervously wrapping her index finger through the curl. Shelly really didn't want to cut her long hair. Her dad was abusive and when he was really angry, he would grab her by the hair and jerk her around. Right now, though, he had left her mom and her to shack up with someone else. Maybe she could keep her long hair while he was gone and she and her Mom could live in peace for awhile. Her head jerked up as one of the hairdressers was putting a lady under the dryer. Shelly could smell the permanent solution as it began to sting her nose.

Shelly let her thoughts drift back to when she and four other senior girls had been invited to Loren Camden's home.

An elegant afternoon tea party was set up in the dining room.

Small fragile tea cups were set at each place. A large plate of several kinds of cookies and little square sandwiches with the crusts cut off were in the middle of the table. A couple of the girls acted like they had been to tea parties before. Shelly inwardly laughed. Who were they kidding? They all came from middle class families and no tea other than iced tea was served in their homes. All of them tried to copy each other in holding their cup and drinking the hot tea like they were used to doing it.

Their thoughts were on those movie magazines they read showing pictures of the actors .sitting around at an elegant table drinking tea and eating the small square sandwiches.

After the tea party, they were ushered into the back sunroom where they sat in comfortable chairs overlooking the pasture behind the home. Loren began by briefly telling the girls about the purpose of inviting them into her home.

She wanted the girls to learn 'lady-like' etiquette from high society. They would learn how to conduct themselves as ladies. Loren told them about visiting the beauty shop in town and Peggy offering to give each girl tips on how to style her hair and apply different make-ups. Everyone was totally in favor of that. They had read society pages and seen actors on TV looking like a million dollars. This just might be their big chance to get out of their 'hick' town. The question, when do we start? Put everyone in agreement. Loren would check with Peggy as to when they could start.

Loren then told them about her 'journey of faith'. Their church was old and uninteresting, stuffy and just plain dull. They just were not interested in that part of their make-over. They would agree to stay with her teaching them as long as possible. Somehow they would stall the 'church' part.

Meeting the street preacher, told Loren, she could have peace with God began her thoughts toward Him. Her journey was really confirmed when she found the Gideon Bible in the woman's lounge at the race track. The picture of Jesus holding the lamb on the rocky hillside brought the desire to find God.

Loren, then told them about her journey across country for two weeks with the two horses, a tent and a book on surviving the outdoors. They listened as if they were being told a fairy tale. Could a person really meet God that way?

Reading from the old Bible the stableman gave her led her to the faith in which God was helping her find. Each episode along the trail in her life brought about finding God through the faith in Jesus Christ. She next introduced them to the Bible and passages about the women in the Bible.

She read some in the book Esther expressing the fact that some of the ancient kings and rulers treasured their women. Even though Esther was the King's wife, she had to be careful on how she approached him. When she found out that her people, the Jews, were going to be in danger of losing their lives, Esther fasted and prayed before she went to see the King. He granted Esther's request and her people were saved. Loren also read Proverbs 14:1 that said: *Every wise woman builds her house, but the foolish woman tears it down with her hands.* Loren also read some of Song of Solomon that is a book full of love that Christ has for His Church. The verses really sounded like a man talking about a woman to Shelly. Each verse sounded so personal!

As Shelly sat there in the beauty shop's chair awaiting her turn, she remembered some of the passages that were read, almost made her face turn red. She never realized that the people in the Bible days were that compassionate with their spouses.

When Loren stepped out of the room for a short while, Shelly had put her hand on the soft leather cover of Loren's Bible. Was there really hope for the future found inside this Book? She had listened as Loren told the story about her journey of faith, as she called it. Taking a two week horseback ride through the wilderness on her way from the city to their town of Waverly, didn't seem that exciting, at least for her. She would never do anything like that. Shelly's mind seemed to suddenly focus on possible journeys she could take on her own.

She was still too young to drive a car. Having money to travel was definitely out of the question. With no job after school and her mom struggling to support the two of them, well, she was sort of stuck. At least for now. If she stayed with these other girls and followed Loren's teaching, maybe there would be a way someday. She also wondered about the boys in her class. She knew that Loren's husband, Andy was going to try to get the boys interested in other things besides girls and video games. She chuckled. Well, good luck with that!

One of the women hairdressers was now free. She called Shelly. Shelly stood up and walked back to the lady's station. She looked over at Janice and was amazed at the change her hairdresser had made. Wow! Won't Brad be surprised to see her now!

Shelly sat down in the chair and the lady put the plastic apron over her, covering her front. She asked Shelly what she would like to have done.

"I was going to have it cut short, but I think I will keep it long. Can you show me a couple easy styles that I can use to put my hair up?"

"Yes, madam. Let me turn you toward the mirror after I wash your hair. Then you can tell me what you think would look best."

Oh, the wonderful feeling of someone else's hands massaging her scalp as the shampoo was applied! As the warm water circulated around her head in the rinsing process, Shelly felt great. The treatment was so relaxing, Shelly had almost been tempted to fall asleep!

Her mother had washed her hair when she was a small child,

but now that she was a teenager, she was on her own in that department.

Now, the hairdresser combed through the long strands removing all the tangles. She put Shelly under the dryer to dry her hair, then brought her back to the chair. There, she demonstrated a couple styles, then guided Shelly's hands to perform the styles herself. Shelly picked one style to stay in her hair as she stepped back over to the chairs by the window. She would wait for Nancy, who was just finishing up with her hairstylist. They could walk home together.

With their hair styles done, a lady took them to the other side of the beauty parlor and began showing them how to apply different make-ups to accent their skin coloring. Even their fingernails were shaped and painted for them. Each girl felt like a million bucks!

They were grateful for Loren's help, but they really weren't sure about the 'Bible' part of this learning process. All decided to stay until it got too 'personal', then they would decide whether to give in to Loren's attempts to lead them towards Jesus or back out while the getting was good.

On their way home, they collected several looks from some of the boys who hung out at the video store. As they passed, a wolf whistle sent them on their way a little faster. Those boys were not good company to be in. Even though their whistles were uplifting, they were not who they wanted to receive compliments from.

Shelly rushed up the stairs to her bedroom, closing the door behind her. Her face flushed with excitement from being whistled at by other teenage boys and feeling so sophisticated. She sat down at her dresser and stared at the different face in the mirror. With well applied make-up, she could *really* pass as an older young lady. Wasn't that what the girls were really trying to accomplish under Loren's tutorage? Out of the corner of her eye, she spotted her neighbor girl in her yard two yards over. So plain! The girl was a year younger, but she didn't seem to have any…. Shelly's conscience began to bother her. The girl needed the same kind of help that she and her friends were receiving from Loren. Maggie was below her standards, though. She would be talked about among her friends if she befriended Maggie. Could helping Maggie be a way to take her 'journey of faith'? Shelly thought to herself; she could only try and see what happens.

Maggie Joiner was a slender willowy junior. None of her dresses fit her properly giving her the shapeless look. She was an 'A' student, but seemed to have no desire to show off in public or aspire in the upper social activities in her school class. Her parents had divorced right after she had been born, leaving her mother to raise her alone. A grandparent had helped out when she was little, but now that she was a teenager, she was almost on her own while her mother worked. Her complexion was smooth, in a heart-shaped face. Bright blue eyes took in her 'dull' surroundings as she hung the last shirt on the line. Maggie looked around at her surroundings. Garbage littered the bottom of the neighboring fence. Maggie wrinkled up her nose. No one seemed to care about keeping their property clean and free of vermin. She didn't have time to do her home chores without having to do what their landlord was supposed to be doing. If no one else cared, why should she?

Never before had Maggie taken stock on what was going on around her. She had been trying to help her mom and keep up her school grades. She had noticed the other girls in the upper grades enjoying themselves on dates, going to parties and stopping in town at the soda fountain for a coke. No one had ever befriended her, so she didn't know what it would be like to do some of the things the other girls did. Even attending a movie seemed like fun, because her mom couldn't afford a TV. Maggie had heard a couple of the senior girls talking in the school hallway about going to the town beauty parlor to learn how to style their hair. Oh, that would have been so much fun!

The soap her mom bought to wash their hair hardly made any suds. Maggie had to use hand lotion, to keep her hands from getting red and chapped. Her shoulders slumped forward, she turned and walked back inside. The vacuuming still had to be done before she started dinner. Her mom would be home soon. Her time of wishing and dreaming was over for now.

Shelly watched Maggie retreat inside her home. How was *she* going to help this girl? Would she join them when they went back out to Loren's? At school the next day, she would ask her even if the others objected.

Shelly got her chance to see Maggie before lunch in the hallway near her locker. Shelly sort of winced as she looked at the ill fitting dress Maggie was wearing. This was not going to be easy.

As Maggie came closer, Shelly stepped out from the lockers to block her way.

"Hello Maggie."

Maggie stopped and stared at the beautiful teenager in front of her. Her mind raced trying to come up with her name. Her mouth opened, but no sound came out.

Shelly tried a weak smile. "I'm Shelly Granger. I live a couple houses over from yours. Are you free tomorrow after school?"

"Why? I'm not in your social click. What do you want with me?"

"I know, but I really want to know you better. Some of my friends have been getting together at Loren Camden's farm for Bible study and learning how to dress and stuff. Loren and her husband are going to work with the teenagers at church. They are trying to find ways to get us to come to church. We have fun. Can you come?"

"You will just make fun of me. I am doing the best I can. Now leave me alone."

Maggie pushed her way past Shelly and headed on down the hall toward her next class. Shelly frowned. That surely didn't go very well.

If Maggie would not go with her and her friends, then she would have to try the one on one tactic. Maybe Maggie would go with her alone to Loren's.

The rest of the day passed as usual. When Shelly got home, she called Loren to see if she could come out alone with a friend. Loren was somewhat surprised, but accepted for the Friday night. Now, if Shelly can get Maggie to go, then she had her start.

Shelly still couldn't understand why the drive in her was so great to do this kind thing for Maggie. She could almost guess what her other friends would think when she started 'hanging out' with an underclassmen, poor dresser and non social person.

At school the next day, Shelly tried again to approach Maggie. This time Maggie reluctantly agreed to go with her Friday afternoon. Maggie let Shelly know that she needed to be home at a certain hour to have dinner ready for her Mom when she came home from work. As Maggie watched Shelly walk away, she wondered why Shelly was doing this. They had nothing in common, other than being close neighbors, oh, and the fact, both had no live-in father.

Deep down though, Maggie felt a spark of excitement grow.

She had been asked to do something totally different. Would she be able to participate in the hairdressings and tea parties she had heard about? She headed off toward her next class, her mind already on her assignment. She dared not think about the next couple of days that would take her closer to Friday. With a little spring in her step, she rounded the corner and entered the classroom.

The next couple of days seemed to drag by. Maggie was getting really excited about going to Loren Camden's after school Friday with Shelly. What would they do? Shelly mentioned Church and a Bible Study. She had thought it was about hairdressing, tea parties and learning how to entertain. Only time would tell. Grabbing the last book from her locker, she closed the door of her locker and took off for her last class of the day.

CHAPTER 6

Andy shifted his briefcase to his other hand as he left the Grayson Electronics building. The government building where he needed to go was only two buildings down. Swinging left on the sidewalk, he began walking. His thoughts were on the prototype chip in his briefcase. If it worked properly the government would purchase it to send to the space station on its next scheduled launch. He was excited, but also a little scared. There were bad characters out there willing to steal the chip to sell to another country. So far only Mr. Grayson and a couple of his loyal staff knew about it. He hadn't even told Loren what he had been working on in his shop at home.

The ride up to the top floor in the elevator seemed cold and spooky. Was he really doing the right thing? Would the government use the chip lawfully? In just a brief second before the elevator doors slid open, did Andy wish he had stuck to making chips for other electronic devices. Silently the doors slid open. Andy stepped out into a large open office. A short balding man in a dark suit stepped forward. He greeted Andy with an outstretched hand. He had been expected. Andy followed the man back through a maze of office cubicles. At the end of the hallway, they entered an ornamental glass etched door. The whole back of the office was in windows overlooking the city sky. Andy instantly thought of people complaining about government waste of good money.

Here, was a good example. Thousands of dollars had been spent on this office alone, not counting the beautiful doorway they had entered through.

Behind the large mahogany wood desk stood a tall slim man with graying hair along the temples. His face looked like it had been chiseled from stone. No sign of emotion cracked that 'stone' until Andy was introduced. A hint of a smile came out. Andy sat down facing the man who now sat down.

"Now, Mr. Camden, let's talk about your computer chip. Tell me what its capability is and how it works."

Andy pulled out the prototype and handed it over to Mr. Browning. At least that is what the name plate on his desk read. The strange feeling about doing this, surrounded Andy's thoughts. He felt lead to hold back some of the information regarding the chip. Why, he really didn't know right then.

"Mr. Camden, when will you be able to demonstrate what

this chip can and will do?"

"We would need to go to Houston or the Space Center in Florida to check with the engineers there. I can make an appointment and get back with you. I still need to make an original chip from this one before any further steps can be done."

"That sounds good. We will send one of our men along to protect you and your property. If this gets out, other countries might try to steal it for their gain."

Mr. Browning stood up and stretched a hand across the desk. Andy stood and shook his hand. Browning hit a buzzer on his desk and the same man came in to escort Andy back to the elevator.

"We'll be in touch. There will be a man waiting by the elevator who will follow you home."

Andy was instantly dismissed. He followed the man back to the elevator. The man nodded farewell, then turned to leave once the elevator doors opened for Andy to get on. The hair on the back of Andy's head seemed to stand up. This was going to be a dangerous situation. Was it going to be safe enough for Loren and Kit? Andy let out a huge sigh. Slowly he took deep breaths to calm himself before the elevator door opened on the lobby floor. His future was now on unsafe grounds.

In the elevator, Andy had time to think about the man going with him back to the house. It would be an inconvenience and also a drawing to him. Andy didn't want to be noticed by the public. Even if he tried to slip by the man waiting for him, they would eventually find him and show up at the farm.

Once outside, the man waiting, was tall and lanky with neatly cut light brown hair and a likeable face. He asked where Andy had parked. Andy told him he had walked down the street from Grayson's Electronics. Together, they walked down the sidewalk past a couple tall buildings. Andy walked around his car to the driver's side and unlocked the car, then got inside behind the wheel. The other man introduced himself after getting into the car on the passenger side.

"My name is Kurt. My car is in the parking garage. I always carry extra clothes and stuff in the trunk. I'm always on the go, so I have to be prepared."

Kurt unwrapped his long legs as they stopped beside his car in the garage. Quickly he retrieved his duffle bag from the trunk, then relocked his car.

"Well, I'm not sure if we have room for you at the house. We only have two bedrooms and our foster son stays in one. We'll work out something after we get there."

Upon arriving at the farmhouse, Andy decided to fix up a bed for the man in his workshop. There, he would be guarding the chip and not be in the way. Kurt would have access to the second bathroom next to the workshop. Andy used it on occasion while he was working in the workshop. Their family life would not be disrupted. They had a spare single bed in the attic that could be brought down and a few other furniture pieces to make it feel like a spare room.

Andy drove around to the back of the house where the workshop was located. Kurt, grabbed his duffle bag from the back seat. then followed Andy inside.

The house was quiet. Both Loren and Kit were gone. Andy noticed both horses were gone, also. Evidently they went riding. He looked in the refrigerator for something to eat. Tuna salad was there along with a couple boiled eggs.

"Are you hungry, Kurt? I have tuna and chips."

"Good. Yes, I am hungry." Kurt found where the paper plates were located and peeled off a couple. Andy set the table with some cold drinks and silverware. At least, the guy didn't seem lazy as he worked along with Andy getting things ready to eat.

Andy surprised him, though, as he said table grace. In his line of work, he had never met someone who actually did that in public. When Kurt was growing up as a youngster, his father often offered up a prayer at the table. This assignment just might be a nice easy one. They ate in silence for the better part of the meal. Near the end, they both heard the voices of Loren and Kit as they sounded excited about their ride. Both stopped short in surprise as they entered the kitchen and saw the stranger sitting at the table with Andy.

"Hello. How long have you been home?" asked Loren as she set down the coffee cup she had retrieved from the barn. She walked over to the kitchen sink, setting down the cup. Kit had opened up the refrigerator door and pulled out the gallon of milk. Loren set two glasses down and let Kit pour milk into both of them. Kit replaced the milk in the refrigerator, then carried the two glasses over to the two empty places at the table. Loren brought a couple paper plates and set them down. Together, they sat down with Andy and Kurt. Both Loren and Kit sat down, looking at Andy, awaiting an introduction.

Andy grinned. "Long enough to devour a sandwich. Do we still have some chocolate chip cookies? Oh, this is Kurt. He's my bodyguard for my computer chip. Kurt, this is my wife, Loren and my foster son Kit."

Kit came over to stand beside Kurt instead of sitting down. "Wow! Are you really a government agent?"

Kurt chuckled. "Not really, kid. This is my first assignment that is even close to being dangerous."

Loren came up beside Andy. "What do you mean, dangerous?"

Andy patted her arm, then smiled up at her. "Now, Loren, it probably won't be anything. We are just taking precautions. Your dad will help all he can, too."

"Just what is it that you have done to make this government

agent guard what you are doing dangerous?"

Andy explained some of the details of the chip, but not everything. The few who knew, the better. Kit was hanging onto every word out of Andy's mouth. He could tell, even though he was just a kid, that everything was not all out on the table. Andy was protecting them. Kit could tell that Loren wasn't buying it, either. Kit looked up at Loren. She read his look. They would play along and see what transpired. Andy explained where Kurt would be staying, then the two went off to the workshop. They started moving tables around to make room for the bedroom items. Kit grabbed a handful of the chocolate chip cookies, then went to his room. He smelled like a horse. He needed a shower.

CHAPTER 7

Friday came all too slow for Shelly. She could hardly wait until the final bell rang and the classes for the week was over. She met Maggie and they walked home together. Their school clothes were changed for everyday outfits, then Shelly got them a ride out to the Camden farm. Loren was waiting for them. She had some cookies and cold iced tea waiting back in the sun room. Maggie looked around and stopped to admire the fall mural on the wall surrounding the fireplace. Loren came up beside her.

"That is where Andy and I got married. Andy had the photograph made into this mural so we will always remember our wedding day. Corny., huh?"

"It's a beautiful place. It looks so peaceful."

"It is. It's the land behind where Andy's parents live. They have a horse stables where they teach kids horseback riding. Now, Shelly, what can I do for you two?"

"Maggie could use some pointers on how to look. My friends would not understand me associating with….."

Maggie jumped into the conversation. "I **am not** a piece of furniture to be talked about behind my back. I am right here."

"We want to improve your potential, Maggie. Shelly wants to help you as do I. Let's come into the sun room here and have some refreshments and get acquainted first."

The three sat down. Loren handed the cool glasses of iced tea to each, then passed the cookies. Maggie told Loren a little about herself as they began. Loren offered to help Maggie select some clothing from pictures in a catalog that she liked. With a few helpful suggestions, Loren told Maggie how to remake her own clothes until she was able to buy new outfits. None of Shelly's clothes would fit her, but some of the accessories like scarves and pins would help. A trip to the beauty parlor was scheduled for Maggie the following Monday after school. There she would learn what the other girls did when they attended to get their beauty treatments.

Maggie began to get a faint glimmer of hope. She wanted to be able to look like some of the other teens, but her clothes selections were slim. Shelly had offered to help. Loren led them in a short prayer, then checked her watch. She needed to get the girls back home. Kit came racing through stopping at the cookie jar. He had been outside in the barn playing with a new litter of kittens. He glanced up at Shelly and Maggie as they were walking past toward the front door. What a difference between the two! Even though Maggie looked plain, he still felt like she could be someone to call a friend.

"Kit, you want to ride to town with us? I'm taking the girls home."

"Sure. Let me wash my hands. We have some new kittens in the barn. I just found them."

Maggie's face lightened up. She loved cats. "Oh I wish I had time to go see them. Do you suppose I could when I come out again?"

"Sure. I'll introduce you to our horse and my pony, too."

"I would like that. I have always wanted to ride a horse."

"Maybe you can someday."

The ride to town was soon over and Loren returned home. Kit was quiet on the way home. He wondered what was going on with all these 'girls' coming out to the house.

"Say, Mom, what's with all the girls coming to the house?"

Loren laughed. "We are teaching them how to be beautiful inside and out. We are offering them something they really want in hopes of getting them to listen to our Bible teachings. The church needs young people and we are working to get them there."

"Yeah, but what about the boys? I seem to be the only one here."

"Andy is working out his schedule to figure out how to

approach the boys. You gave us some excellent suggestions, though."

"Andy seems a little worried about that new chip he just made. He told me he was taking it to the government after talking to your dad."

"I suppose so. He hasn't really talked much about it. Probably top secret."

"I hope it won't be dangerous for us."

"Me, too."

Several weeks went by with no trouble at the farmhouse or other places Andy would have gone. Kit was home alone up in the hay loft counting the bales of hay. Andy needed to know how many were up there so he would know when to order another load. Kit stopped by the window to wipe the sweat off his forehead. Out of the corner of his eye, he saw something flash by the house. Quickly he turned to look out the window. Down in the yard a green jeep was driving slowly around behind the house. Where had it come from? Surely Ranger would have neighed if the jeep had come up the front driveway. Kit knew that Andy had the chip with him because he had gone to Loren's father's company to get spare parts. Kurt had gone with them. The two men who got out of the jeep were strangers. Kit heard Ranger snorting in the corral. If he could get down the back way and let Ranger out... Ranger might go up to the house and surprise those trespassers. Quickly Kit climbed down the ladder and slipped out the back door. Ranger saw him come out and nickered. Kit lifted the latch on the corral gate and motioned for Ranger to come out. With the gate swung wide, Ranger trotted out. He nudged Kit as if asking what he was supposed to do. Kit stretched out his arm, pointing up towards the house. Ranger tossed his head, then took off toward the house. Kit closed the gate so his pony wouldn't come out, too. He moved around through the trees and brush to watch.

Ranger scared the two men when they came back out of the workshop. Their search was in vain. No computer chip or drawings were available to snatch.

Ranger bumped them around with his shoulders and rump. Several times they fell down from being pushed off balance.

One tried to hit Ranger who in turn, sunk his teeth into the man's arm. With a yell, they tried to get into their jeep. Both of them rolled their windows up so Ranger would not stick his nose in and bite. With the grinding of the gears, the jeep leaped forward and headed back toward the opening in the fence behind the house that they had made.

Kit scratched the license plate number in the dirt with a stick. He heard the jeep start up. It didn't drive down the driveway, but went through the woods behind the house and bounced along across the back pasture. Kit scratched his head, puzzled. They had fixed that fence last week. Had those two men cut the wire to get onto the property? Kit hadn't seen how the men had come up to the house. They must have come through the back pasture and cut the fence as they got to the house. As he watched the jeep across the pasture, he thought maybe he could follow them. Ranger came back to the corral. Kit had his pony out throwing on the saddle. Ranger was closed back into the corral with the latch firmly replaced.

"Good job, boy. We got them on the run. Now, I'm going to see if I can find out where they are going. Has to be another break in our back fence. Hope the cows don't get out on the highway over there. See you later!"

Kit climbed into the saddle and kicked the pony in the ribs. It jumped forward and off they went. Kit was hanging on tight until he picked up the pony's rhythm. Loren had been helping him ride faster. Once more he felt like a real cowboy riding fast over the country. He quickly reined the pony behind a huge bush.

He was getting too close to the jeep. The jeep was near the new break in the fence the men had made and was slowly driving out. They stopped on the outside and one of them got out to pull the fence back up. Kit watched as they looped a piece of wire over the post to hold the fence up. This was where they had come out. They turned to the left going farther down the dirt road. Kit grinned. He knew where that road went. He and Loren had ridden alongside it just that morning. They had not seen the break in the fence then. Slowly Kit rode among the trees as he stayed in the pasture being careful not to be seen by the men in the jeep.

They had gone quite a ways before the jeep stopped as it approached a black limousine. Kit pulled the pony to a stop. Carefully he sought shelter from their view behind a huge clump of bushes. He was too far away to hear any conversation. When the limousine left, he might be able to get the license plate number before heading for home. Kit dismounted and looped the reins over a branch on the bush. Crouching down, he wove around through the brush to get a better look at seeing the license plate on the limo. Whoever was inside the limo did not come out or show themselves. Just as Kit had scratched off the numbers and letters on the license plate, the jeep raced its engine causing it to backfire. Kit jerked up his head in time to see his pony take off. The men paid no attention to it as they climbed back into their vehicles. Everyone left the scene. Both the limo and jeep turned around and drove back toward the main highway. Kit stayed hidden until the coast was clear. He rewrote the license number onto a piece of pine bark. He would have to carry it very carefully so it wouldn't break apart.

Now, to get back home! He knew he was a long way from the back pasture fence by the barn. He cut through the brush in an effort to make a shortcut.

Back at the farmhouse, Andy and Kurt discovered that someone had broken into the workshop. They saw the jeep tracks and horse prints around the back door. Footprints told them there had been some kind of a struggle. Ranger was back in his corral. Somehow he had gotten out and surprised the intruders.

"What is with your horse? Is he some kind of watch-dog?"

"Yes. He lets us know if a stranger comes on the property. Kit is missing as is his pony. I'll bet he tried to follow whoever it was. There. I hear a horse running. Come on."

They hurried down toward the stable in time to see the pony come up to the pasture fence without Kit. Its reins were hanging down with pieces of brush caught near the end. Andy opened the gate and led the pony inside. He tied it to the fence.

"Kit is out there on foot somewhere. I'll ride out and see if I can save him the long walk home. See you later, Kurt."

Andy took Ranger out of the corral and vaulted onto his back. Without saddle or bridle, he guided the horse through the gate and on into the pasture. Kurt watched him go, then thought he would help by unsaddling the pony. When he had finished, he started back toward the house when he noticed the scratching in the dirt near a tree. With a closer look, he saw the numbers and letters that could be from a license plate.

Taking his notebook and pen from his pocket, he wrote them down, then called his boss on the cell phone.

Kit leaned up against a tree, then slid down to the ground. He was tired! How long he had walked, he didn't know. He had just stretched out his legs when he heard a horse coming. Looking back toward the farmhouse, he saw someone riding Ranger coming toward him! Hot dog! A ride home! Slowly he scrambled to his feet, dusting off the leaves from his pants. Holding up a hand, he waved, getting a wave back. Ranger slowed to a stop a few feet from where Kit stood. Andy smiled down at him.

"Someone call for a ride?"

"Yes, sir! A car backfired and scared the pony. I wasn't on him, either, so I didn't get thrown off."

"Okay. Let's get you on board, then you can tell me what you are doing way out here."

Andy slid off and helped Kit climb onto Ranger's back, then vaulted onto his back behind Kit. Ranger turned around and started walking toward home. Kit told him about seeing two men in a jeep go into the workshop. He had turned Ranger loose to go scare them a bit. He then had saddled the pony and followed them out to a dirt road where they had cut the fence and put it back up when they had gone back out. He showed Andy the piece of pine bark that he had written the limo's license plate number on.

Kit was so engrossed in his adventure that he really didn't think about being on top of Ranger riding bareback. He was on a full grown horse for the first time! Slowly he let his gaze look down, seeing the great distance it was to the ground. He sure didn't relish the thought of falling off from way up there! Being up on the pony's back was high enough.

Now safely back home and after another shower to clean up, Kit was ready for a nice quiet time stretched out on the couch watching TV. Andy and Kurt met in the workshop to discuss the events of the day. Someone from the government office was checking the DNV of the two vehicles. Soon, they would know who the men were in the cars. The chip needed more security. Mr. Grayson was called and arrangements were made for them to have a place there at Grayson Electronics to complete the computer chip. With the possibilities of having it around was becoming dangerous. This way there would be more people around for security and less chance of someone trying anything to steal the chip.

Andy got out the dominoes and set them up on a card table. Kurt sat down and began turning them over to start a game. They needed time to calm down. Loren would be home soon and they really didn't want her to know what had just happened. Kit was back at work in the barn completing the chores Andy had assigned him to earlier. The kittens frolicked around the bales of hay causing Kit to watch them instead of working. The Mom cat watched everything from her high perch on top of the bales of hay.

CHAPTER 8

One of the girls in Shelly's group found out about Shelly hanging out with Maggie, a lower classman. Soon, all five seniors turned their noses up at Shelly when she tried to join them for lunch. School would be out soon for the summer and they usually planned out their summers together. This summer, however, would be different because they were all seniors, graduating. No more school for them; at least for those not going on to college in the fall. Shelly felt the cold stares of the girls as she carried her lunch tray over toward their table. As she got closer, the girls already sitting down, moved around, leaving no room for her to sit.

"What gives?"

"You have been seen in undesirable company."

"You mean Maggie? She's on the honor roll in her junior class."

"That is not the problem. She dresses funny and seems to

work at home all the time. She doesn't party or hang out where we do."

"She doesn't have the money to do that. Her mother works all day and someone has to do the homemaking jobs after school. All I did was to show her how we changed our hair styles at the beauty parlor and used some scarves and pins to change our appearance."

"Well, if you want to stay with us, drop her."

"If she were dressed like us, would you consider letting her visit Loren with us?"

The girls exchanged looks among themselves. No, they would not consider this lower classmate. "It is either us or her." They told Shelly. It would take more than a clothes change to make them change their minds. Maggie would have to party, spend money and get into the group with their activities. Shelly knew Maggie could not do this. She was practically poor like she was. The other girls did not know of Shelly's home situation or they would probably kick her out of their 'little group', too. So far Shelly had had money to spend with them on their outings.

Shelly returned home really depressed. This 'Christian journey' seemed almost too much to stand. Wasn't there a Bible scripture Loren had shared with her that said that God does not put more on us than what we can stand? Just the thought of knowing that instantly raised her spirits. The knowledge that all of her friends were going to drop her from their group seemed to hurt the most. She had enjoyed being with the popular girls and being around all those handsome jocks who were in their group. Her life seemed to be changing and her old friends didn't seem as important to her now. Now being one of Jesus' followers seemed to change her place with her social friends.

Up in her room, she dug out her yearbook and flipped through it to find Maggie's classmates. She wondered if any of them were in the same situation as Maggie. Why in no time she could have a group of her own to help. She opened her desk drawer and pulled out paper and a pen. With the names of Maggie's classmates, she wrote down a dozen names to start with. She could notify these or have Maggie help and start something new. Excitement bubbled through her.

She felt her 'mission' coming together. What had Loren said? 'All things are possible with Christ.' Shelly moved her finger down the telephone page until she found the name she was seeking. Dialing it, she held her breath as the party she wanted to speak with answered. Slowly Shelly told her why she had called. Would she be interested in joining Maggie and her in a group to learn hair styles, make-up and learn what God had in store for them if they accepted Him.

After getting three more calls and excited responses, she called Loren. Loren would have to know so she could plan something for this new group. Loren was equally excited. This was going far better than she had hoped. Maybe these new girls would be just as easy to 'train' as Shelly's group.

Shelly hadn't told Loren about her being shunned from her group. They made plans for everyone in Maggie's group to meet at the Malt Shop after school the next day.

Andy came home weary from being at Grayson Electronics all day long. Kurt was equally as tired and promptly crashed in the nearest chair to the front door. Andy dropped his briefcase on the coffee table, then sat on the couch. Loren had heard them coming in and brought out two iced glasses of iced tea with lemonade mixed together. All of the cookies had been devoured by Kit. Loren put some store-bought cookies on a plate and brought it out along with a glass of iced tea for herself.

"I see you both have had a rough day at the office. I have some news. Shelly has rounded up another group of girls from the junior class and wants to meet tomorrow after school. I guess you haven't had much time to try for the boys yet."

Andy shook his head. "This chip for the space program is driving me batty. I just get it to working great in the workshop, then take it to Grayson's and poof, it doesn't work. I might have to rebuild the chip there at Grayson's. Say, you worked in the assembly part. Maybe you can figure it out for me here in the shop."

"I just might, but all the equipment I would need is probably there at Grayson's. I have a beef and noodle casserole in the oven. It will be ready in about a half hour. If you two want to get cleaned up, I'll see if I can find Kit."

Loren found Kit in the corral with both horses. Ranger was getting a good ear scratch with the pony waiting patiently near-by for his. Loren stopped by the gate and watched the three. Grinning, she felt blessed to have a young man who could get along with her horse. The pony's ears flipped forward as it saw Loren standing there. Kit turned around, stopping the ear scratching. Ranger bumped him with his nose, as if to say, 'why did you stop?' Kit laughed.

"Hi, Loren. Did you need me for something?"

"Not really. I have dinner almost done and came out to have you come on in. We can do the chores afterwards."

"I did catch the cow and it's inside the barn ready to be milked. Andy hasn't gotten around to showing me how to do it yet."

Loren laughed. "It's fun. Where's Tom?"

'Waiting. He's almost gotten the kittens to wait in line, too. You won't believe what those cats are doing."

"Come on. I've got to see this."

Loren left the fence and headed for the barn door. Kit slipped under the rails and joined her. His pony neighed as if to say, 'What happened to My ear scratching?"

Tom, the tomcat, heard the barn door open and saw Loren

and Kit enter. He made a low meow, then waited. Four kittens scampered out from one of the empty stalls and stood beside him. Loren shook her head in amazement as she took the stool and milk bucket to the cow. She sat down on the stool.

"Kit, I'll feed the cats first and you watch. Then, I will let you have a go at the milking."

Kit watched the hilarious display the cats put on as they sat ready to receive the stream of milk from the cow. He put a hand over his mouth to keep from laughing out loud and maybe scaring the cats. The kittens jostled for position as Loren aimed the cow's teat toward the kittens, the milk stream splashing all over them. Old Tom and 'his lady' had had their fill and were waiting for the kids to enjoy the milky treat. Kit moved over to the stool and took his seat. Slowly he reached out to take hold of the cow's teats. Loren instructed him on the pressure of his hands and the pulling down to draw out the milk. Kit almost jumped off the stool as he succeeded to land the first spray into the bucket. He picked up the rhythm as he listened to the milk spray hitting the bottom of the bucket. When he glanced around, all of the cats were gone. The kittens were busy investigating a chameleon crawling around a feed tub. Loren was dishing out grain for the horses and pony.

Kit heard Ranger neigh, then the sound of a strange car coming up the gravel driveway.

He couldn't leave his job or see the car from where he sat.

Loren had come back into the barn and watched the car approach the house. She motioned for Kit to come to her. Kit got up from the stool and pulled the partially filled milk bucket from under the cow, setting it down out of the cow's way. He quickly made his way to Loren's side. He saw the jeep. It looked like the one that he had seen on the road. The hairs on the back of his neck stood up.

"Where is Andy? That is the same car that was here before. He needs to get out of there fast! Let me get Ranger."

"He's in the workshop." Loren reached over to the phone by the back door. Quickly she buzzed the house. Andy answered the phone. "Andy, danger. Get out of there!" Loren hung up the phone and turned around to Kit who was not there!

Kit had gone out the back door and opened the corral gate for Ranger to come out.   Ranger came out and stood waiting for Kit to tell him to go.

"Back door, Ranger! Get Andy!"

Ranger leaped into action and raced to the back door of the house. Andy and Kurt were just coming out as Ranger came to a halt. Kurt vaulted onto Ranger's back followed by Andy. The two raced back to the barn and slid off. Together all of them watched the house. The two men came out the back door and looked around, seeing nothing. Ranger had walked on the grass, leaving no tracks to be seen.

A few minutes later, the men came through the front door,

returned to the jeep then drove back toward the main road the way they had come. They hadn't thought of searching the barn. Loren and Andy looked at each other. What kind of danger were they in? Kit went back to finish milking the cow. Kurt used his cell to call his office to report the visit.

After hanging up the phone, Kurt turned to Andy. "You are going to have to move your workshop to Grayson Electronics. You are in danger here and putting your family in danger too. Let's get started going over everything and deciding what you will need to take."

The smell of the casserole wafted through the doorway. Andy's stomach rumbled. He chuckled, and motioned for Kurt to follow him into the kitchen. The moving could wait whereas the stomach would not.

CHAPTER 9

Loren drove over to the church where Andy was working with the pastor. As Loren got out of her car, she looked around the church yard seeking the pastor and Andy. Back in the very back of the playground area, she saw them.

In the play area, Kit sat on the ground with a big hairy dog romping around him. The dog looked to be almost as tall as Kit if it stood up on its hind legs. Loren watched as the dog pounced on Kit knocking him flat, then pinning him down to commence licking his face. Kit laughed flailing his arms in a feeble attempt to ward off the dog's apparent affection. Andy and the pastor were now standing together near their finished project watching Kit. Loren walked up and quietly stood beside the two men. After a few seconds, Andy turned toward her.

"Hello, honey."

"Where did that huge dog come from? Is he yours, pastor?"

Pastor Raymond laughed. "It's a stray. Someone passing through town, I guess, just up and left him. Probably eating them out of house and home. Jeanie and I have been taking care of him. He seems to love kids, but most of the smaller ones are afraid of him because he's so big."

"Kit seems to get along okay with him."

"Yep. Interested in acquiring a dog? It might make a good watch dog."

Andy laughed. "That big ugly thing wouldn't hurt a flea. Look at Kit. He can put his arm in its mouth and it just comes out wet and slobbery."

At the end of their visit, the dog happily sat in the back of Andy's pick-up truck as they drove back to the farm. Kit kept looking out the back window to make sure the dog wouldn't jump or fall out. He now had a dog. Someone to play with when he wasn't riding his pony. Kit leaped out and called to the dog who jumped to the ground. Slowly it surveyed its surroundings.

Was this going to be his new home? Wow! Look at all the room to run! Without a glance back at Kit, it took off toward the barn and pasture beyond. Kit was ready to yell at it to come back, then thought to just let it run. It needed to see where he was and get acquainted with the surroundings. Kit looked up at Andy and Loren, a grin threatening to spread across his face. This was just perfect! He had a home, a horse and a dog! A perfect combination for a growing boy. He took off running toward the barn, the direction of where the dog went. There were new kittens in the barn and he didn't want the dog bothering them. Loren and Andy went on up to the house and inside.

Loren went into the kitchen and started getting some iced tea and putting ice in the glasses. She carried them back into the living room where Andy sat as he waited for her.

Loren told Andy about the meeting she had planned with the younger girls in the soda shop. They would need to really entice the girls's desires to really want to be a part of their program. So far, Andy had not been able to find time to talk to any of the teenage boys.

They seemed to be invisible whenever he ventured to the spots where Andy knew they hung out. Kit knew how to get them. He had been in the video arcade shop where they all wasted their money in the game machines. Andy had talked to the owner about setting aside a night for free games for the boys. Right then, the asking price was too high. Andy backed off. He needed another tactic for the store owner. He had talked to a couple of the boys and they didn't seem interested to waste their summer learning how to make stuff out of wood. If Andy was offering them use of a basketball court and schedule games with the other high school teens, then they just might follow along with Andy's plan. That had been the project the Pastor and Andy were working on when Loren showed up at the church. The City Park next to the church had a full size basketball court along with a softball field. Waverly might not be a very big town to compete with the city, but they had a state of the art park equipped with all types of equipment for sports and fun.

Would the boys like baseball too? Ideas ran rapid through Andy's head. He needed to get everything written down.

Once inside, Loren grabbed their notebook and its clipboard and sat down on the couch. Andy sat down beside her. They could now begin to formulate their plans for the teens. Ideas were written down and avenues for them to go. The pastor was going to explain their plan to the deacons and elders at their next meeting. Funds were needed to be raised to finance these extra activities at the park. Summer would soon be here and with the summer months ahead, their plans would soon come together.

Loren told Andy about the planned meeting with some of the junior girls, friends of Shelly. They seemed interested in becoming like the seniors who Loren was tutoring.

The next day would tell the outcome of this new group of teens.

Loren walked into the soda shop and instantly spotted the large table full of young teenage girls. She could tell right away that they all could really use some help in their appearance. Shelly spotted her and stood up, grabbing a spare chair from the near-by table. All of the girls stopped talking as they watched the well dressed woman approaching their table.

"Hello, girls. I'm Loren Camden."

Shelly held the chair for her, then took her seat in the booth. Nervously she rubbed her sweaty hands along her slacks. She introduced the girls to Loren. Loren offered her hand to shake to each one to let them know she was glad to meet them.

"I understand from Shelly that all of you are interested in becoming, how should I say it, more grown-up looking. We can easily do that for you if you are willing to keep it up and do what is necessary to fulfill your expectations. With summer coming on and school closing, your time will be easier to fill with the program. What would you all like to do first?"

"We know that the older classmates spent time in the beauty parlor." the girl looked at the others to affirm the decision. "We have the whole summer ahead of us, so... I guess learning how to arrange our hair might be a good start."

The other girls nodded in total agreement. They wanted to look beautiful.

Loren grinned. This group of girls might be easier to work with than the seniors were. The seniors, Shelly's classmates, seemed to be already getting 'stuck-up.' They just seemed to want the 'outward' appearance to impress the boys.

The Bible study and church attendance part of Loren's

program was for the 'birds'. They would follow Shelly as long as they could get help and tips for nothing.

Loren surveyed all the girls. All of them seemed eager to start their transformation from dull to beautiful. Some of the senior girls did it, so they could too.

"Okay. I'll set up a date with the beauty shop and let you know when. Saturdays are their busiest day. Can all of you meet someday during the week? After school before school is out?"

"Thursdays are good for most of us."

"Good. I'll go see Peggy after we finish here. Did Shelly tell you what else I am doing for her classmates?"

Loren was greeted with confused stares. No, Shelly hadn't told them anything, other than a beauty shop treatment and tips on preparing for a party.

Not to scare any of them off, Loren slowly approached the subject of the church. They were not really sure if they wanted to attend church. Loren took out a small New Testament and opened it to some scripture.

"How many of you know anything about the Bible?"

"It's a story book about ancient people having wars, fighting and struggling to live."

"What does the Bible have to do with what we want to do?"

"The whole idea behind this beauty project is to show all of you how to be beautiful both inside and out. Our outward appearance should show people what we are like inside. Anger and hatred cannot be hidden very well and will soon leak out to spoil everything we have worked so hard to accomplish. Just having a nice hair style and wearing fancy clothes does nothing for how we are on the inside. Hopefully, I will be able to direct and train all of you who really want to learn everything to get your life on track and in good standing with God."

The girls were silent. Part of them wanted to rebel against this 'religion' stuff Loren was telling them about. Each of the girls seemed to be searching their hearts for an answer that seemed to evade their thoughts. A waitress came over and each girl ordered a milkshake.

Loren tentatively spoke to the girls again. "Do all of you have a Bible at home?"

"I'm sure we do." They replied, nodding their heads and turning their attention back to Loren.

"Will all of you be willing to look up some scripture verses I will write down for you. After reading them, get back to Shelly or Maggie with what you think about continuing our time together."

Loren began to take out her notepad and pen. She copied the same verses out on six sheets and handed them to each of the girls. To the girls, it looked like Greek for all they knew. Maybe one of their parents would know about the Bible, at least enough to help them find the verses. Proverbs, Song of Solomon, St. John and who?

Inwardly they shivered from non-belief. They stole a look at Shelly, then Maggie. Both seemed confident that this would not be 'painful'. It would be like homework. Look up the verses and write them down after reading them.

The milkshakes arrived and everyone was quiet while they drank their shakes. Shelly and Maggie were nervous about this whole thing. Would the others agree to go ahead with Loren and her help to make them more attractive? The answer would be in the next couple of days while each girl searched out the scriptures Loren had given them.

Loren put down her pen and paper. "Let me tell you about myself. My life was boring to the point that I didn't have any ambition at all. I tried every sport and activity to find happiness, but nothing seemed to satisfy my desires. My newest activity was horseback riding. After learning to ride a horse, I had decided to take a two week horseback camping trip to hopefully get my life in order and find out God's plan for my life.. God seemed to be directing me to go and experience life outside of my pampered life. When I met Andy's dad at the horse stables, he gave me an old Bible to read while I took my two week journey. I was a greenhorn and sometimes scared at being alone in the darkness.

At each campsite I made along the trail, I read a little in the Bible and prayed. I found great comfort in doing that each night. When large obstacles stood in my way, it seemed that Jesus was right there beside me. This is not a religion. It is a personal relationship with Jesus. He is our Friend, our Comforter, Someone to call upon for help. He answers the prayers of His children. Even though you do not know how to pray, try to just talk out your thoughts and fears, telling Him what you want Him to do for you. Praying is not hard. It's like talking to a friend.   Let Maggie know if you want to continue this program. I am more than willing to help you. Finding where you stand with Jesus is the main factor of this program I am presenting to you. Just being beautiful on the outside will not cut it in this world we live in now. You all will need to learn how to resist the many temptations offered to you as you live your daily lives. I want to be there to help each and every one of you. You are bound to come upon someone who will pretend to like you, but will be there to hurt or destroy you. Please look up these scriptures and plan on meeting here again next week. In the meantime, I will set up a beauty appointment for you on a Thursday."

With all of the girls leaving the soda shop, Loren followed them out and went to her car. Neither Maggie or Shelly came over to talk, but stayed with the girls as they began their walk home.

All the way home, Loren prayed. Somehow, this new group of teens was going to be difficult. They all seemed set in their ways and wanted no part of church.

Maybe Shelly and Maggie could shed some light on the subject if someone questions them later.

Andy looked up from his newspaper as she came in the front door.

"How'd it go with the girls?"

"They are going to be hard nuts to crack. The minute I mentioned the Bible and church, they clammed up and were ready to run. Hopefully Shelly and Maggie can get them to understand the program that I am trying to present. Time will tell. I gave them some scripture verses to look up if they even know what a Bible is and if they even have one available to them. We just need to pray harder."

Back in town, Shelly was having a serious talk with her 'friends'. She was trying to convince them that Maggie and her friends would not come between them and her. They were now undecided about how they felt about Shelly being with Maggie and the juniors sharing Loren. Shelly had looked up some of the Bible verses Loren had given all of them. There was really more to 'this Christian' way of life than she had thought. Even though the way seemed rough and hard, she was determined to continue and do her 'journey of faith'. With her laptop on her lap, she keyed in 'Women of The Bible'. When all the faces of the women came onto the screen, she raised her eyebrows in surprise. Wow! Thirty-six in the Old Testament and Fifteen in the New! Some of the women's names she recognized. Reaching for her Bible, she began searching for the scripture telling her about particular women.

She chose five to begin with, then went back to read about

each one. Some only had a small part in their lives to contribute to the situations around them, but was known for it. Would God remember her after she had completed her 'journey'?

Shelly chose Ruth. Ruth had left her homeland to stay with her mother-in-law after her husband, her mother-in-law's son had died. They traveled into Naomi's country of Judah, back where she had lived. There, Ruth tried to be accepted by the Jews, her being a Moabite. Shelly thought about herself. What would she have done? Would she have gone back to her own people? Ruth had loved her mother-in-law, Naomi and wanted to be with her.

The choice to change friends and a new lifestyle was now at hand. This was going to require a lot of prayer! Shelly was determined to follow through no matter how hard the 'trail' became.

Shelly knelt down beside her bed and offered up her prayer for help. She let the tears run feely as she told Jesus everything. Somehow everything would work out, maybe not to her satisfaction, but in His time, His will be done. She got off her knees with a new resolve. She would try to help out more around the house for her mother, then make her plans to continue helping Maggie and her friends. Her mother would soon be home from work. What could she fix for their evening meal? Shelly fairly danced down the stairs with a lighter heart and new look for the future.

CHAPTER 10

Maggie twirled around in front of her cracked dresser mirror, grinning at the new image smiling back at her. She had accomplished one of the new hair styles the beautician had shown her. The multicolored scarf draped loosely around her neck added color to the drab colored olive dress. She had managed to sew a couple of tucks in the waistline to make it fit better. With some new shoes that Shelly had given her, she felt like a million bucks!

She heard her mother stirring in the kitchen. Grabbing her schoolbag, she fairly skipped out of her room and down the stairs. Her mother looked at her with wide eyes. Was this really her daughter?

"Maggie, what on earth?" Slowly she came forward to closely inspect Maggie.

"You…. Look beautiful!" Reverently her mother placed her hands on Maggie's face, cupping her chin. She saw the sparkle in

Maggie's eyes. Her girl had changed!

"Thanks, Mom. One of my new school friends loaned me this scarf and Loren Camden took five of us to the beauty shop where the beauticians showed us different hair styles to use at home."

"How much did all this cost? You know we can't afford any of it."

Maggie shook her head. "No, Mom. Loren Camden is trying to help all of us to improve our outlook by some simple tricks of wearing our hair and scarves.

She is trying to get all of us interested in attending Church. I'm so sure it will work, but everyone who is willing will at least try."

"I'd like to meet this woman sometime. Well, here's breakfast such as it is. Suppose they could teach you how to make tuna fish and baloney more tasty?"

Maggie laughed as she sat down to eat the meager breakfast.

"She just might, Mom. Which one is for my lunch today?"

"Say, you can have your pick today. We happen to have both in the refrig."

Maggie went to the refrigerator and pulled out items for her lunch. In a few minutes she had everything she needed. Her mom brought over a big apple to add to her lunch. Maggie thought about all those other girls at school. She was willing to bet that none of them had a loving mother like she did. Sure, they were poor as church mice, but the love that held them together was more than the comforts that more money could buy.

As she was rolling down the top of her lunch bag, she looked over at her Mom. For the first time, Maggie noticed the dark circles around her eyes. When her Mom walked, she noticed the weariness in her strides. She was just being overworked trying to hold them together as a family. Maggie knew she could do no more than she was already to help. Her school grades had to stay up so she could graduate the following year. Her ambitions of attending college were dim. There was barely enough money in their budget to go from month to month without any utility bills being raised.

Shelly had told her that Loren was trying to lead all of the girls to Church and accepting Jesus Christ into their lives. Loren had told Maggie and her friends about her 'journey of faith'. Hopefully they all would realize the importance of taking a journey of faith on their own.

Everyone was different and would be called by the Holy Spirit differently. The Holy Spirit would be the one to convict their hearts to accept Jesus.

Maggie just then realized that was what Shelly was trying to do with her and her friends! Shelly had chosen Maggie as her journey of faith! Wow! Maggie felt right then as if the whole burden of just living was lifted from her back! Shelly hadn't been looking down on her and her friends in a hurtful way. Maggie had noticed the changes in Shelly's friends toward Shelly. Could that be a problem? Maybe they were jealous of Maggie's friends and wanted Shelly all to themselves. But Maggie noticed a change in Shelly. If Shelly stayed true to her new found faith in God, her choice of friends would change also if they didn't believe in God, too.

In the school hallway, several boys in Maggie's class whistled at her as she opened up her locker. Secretly she grinned as she gathered up her books for her first class, then put her lunch bag into the locker. She received other stares, some of admiration and others of surprise for the change in her appearance. Maggie didn't see Shelly until lunch that day when they all went to the cafeteria.

Shelly carried her tray of food over to the table where Maggie was sitting with her lunch bag. "Mind if I join you?"

"Yes, Shelly. How are you today?"

"Not too good. I feel like I am on a desert island and there is no one around. Right now I feel like I can say things to you and you won't snub me. It is hard to continue in my old way of life with my friends."

"I thought you had chosen a new way of life. One closer to Jesus."

"I really want to, but all of my 'so-called' friends are, treating me like I have the plague."

"With all you tried to do to help them with Ms. Camden's

help? The beauty shop and at her home? What did they expect from you?"

Shelly rubbed her hands across her face. "I don't know. I have prayed about it and no answer. This whole thing is taking my concentration from my schoolwork. I have a huge science test coming up next period."

Maggie reached her hands across the table and took hold of both of Shelly's.

"Then we pray harder." Maggie squeezed Shelly's hands with a look of determination on her face.

Shelly looked surprised at her new friend as she bowed her head and listened as Maggie prayed for both of them, but especially for Shelly and her upcoming test. A warm feeling engulfed Shelly as she listened to Maggie pray. The peace found only by trusting in God wrapped her in His warm embrace. A settled peace surrounded both of them.

When she opened her eyes, no one was nearby to hear the prayer or were watching the two of them. They were almost alone in the lunchroom. Shelly looked up at the large clock on the wall. She had fifteen minutes to eat and go get her books from her locker. Shelly looked at what Maggie was eating. Tuna fish! She had wanted one for a long time.

Shelly smelled the tuna sandwich as her mouth started to crave the tuna.

"Uh, Maggie, any chance you would trade lunches with me? You don't know how long I have been craving a tuna sandwich. Mom is allergic to fish so we don't have any fish in the house."

Maggie gave her a lopsided grin. "And just what do you have to offer in exchange for my tuna fish?"

Shelly chuckled. "How about a nice fat roast beef with a double layer of Swiss cheese?"

"Oh that would be yummy! How about sharing my apple? Mom always gives me one and it is always too big."

"Sold!"

The girls laughed together as they traded lunches and quickly began to eat.

Several of Shelly's 'friends' walked past them going out the main door, but only gave them a glance. They couldn't understand Shelly. Just because Maggie had changed her outward appearance, she was the same inside; undesirable to them.

As Shelly sat at her desk with the science test in front of her, the answers seemed to be right on the tip of her tongue. Her pen could hardly keep up with her thoughts as it wrote out the answers. Multiple choice questions were not on this particular test. Fill in the blanks questions took up the whole test. A person had to know the answers in order to pass the test.   Silently she prayed a thank you to God for helping her out and of course, Maggie for her part in praying. Somehow her other problems with 'her friends' would work out, too. She would go out to the farm and visit Loren and maybe Maggie could go with her. Pushing that train of thought back, she refocused on the test.

Her next period was another test. The end of the school year was coming. She needed to make good grades.   As she walked down the hall toward her next class, Maggie was walking the other way toward her class. Shelly gave her a thumbs up sign with a huge smile to go with it. Maggie returned the sign with her smile, then walked on.

When Shelly's friend, Diane, stopped the car in front of Loren's home to drop Shelly and Maggie off, they saw Loren and Kit out at the barn. As they got out of the car, they were attacked by a big dog who jumped upon them, giving both girls a good tongue licking. Diane waited with the car just in case the girls needed to climb back in to escape the overly friendly dog. Laughing and trying to wipe the slobbers from their faces, they scratched at the dog's head. With its huge hairy tail swinging back and forth, it went back down on all fours. One of its ears cocked up and it turned toward the barn where Kit was whistling for it. Maggie and Shelly both looked down at their jeans. The dog had walked through water leaving dog prints on both girls.

Thankfully they had gone home after school and changed before coming to the farm.

Shelly waved goodbye to her friend as she turned the car

around and left.

Loren waved a greeting at them from the barn. She was busy getting ready to milk the cow. As Maggie and Shelly came into the barn, they saw the kittens scrambling about as if they were lining up for something special. Two older cats sat back overseeing their 'kids'.

"Hello girls. Welcome to the cow milking show. Stand over there so you won't get caught in the milk spray. I'll be done in a little while."

Loren set the stool down and stuck the bucket under the cow's teats. Looking back toward the kittens, she squeezed a teat aiming it toward the kittens sending out a spray of milk. Maggie and Shelly laughed at the scene before them. Each kitten got enough of the squirt and then scampered away to lick the milk off themselves.

The two adult cats took their places and accepted their turn with a squirt. Kit came over to Loren. "Let me do the milking. You have company."

"Why thank you, Kit. You know about that batch of warm chocolate chip cookies in the kitchen, don't you?"

Kit grinned. "Yes, Ma'm." He took his place on the stool and began the process of milking. Maggie and Shelly listened to the sound of the milk hitting the bottom of the bucket. Neither girl had seen a cow being milked.

Slowly they followed Loren out of the barn and up to the

house.

"I see the dog greeted you both." laughed Loren looking at the muddy dog prints on the front of their jeans and shirt.

"Yes. We are glad we changed out of our school clothes before coming out. We hope we are not bothering you."

"Not at all. I don't get much company way out here. I have some cold lemonade and of course, the chocolate chip cookies. I seem to be able to make cookies without burning them. I am still learning how to cook different foods to keep my husband happy."

"My mom always told me the wife never cooks as good as the husband's mother."

"That is true. Andy had my parent's cook come out for a couple of days and she taught me how to cook several things. I am still working on pie dough and meat loaf."

They walked into the coolness of the living room. After sitting down, Loren went in the kitchen to fetch the glasses of lemonade and a plate of cookies.

When she returned and set everything down, she waited for one of the girls to speak.

"Now what can I do for you girls?"

Shelly told her about being snubbed by her friends, the ones who had come out there a couple weeks ago. They wanted a make over that Loren gave them all at no expense or strings attached. As far as reading their Bibles and praying, that part never happened and probably would not take place, at least right now.

Loren listened. Everything seemed to have changed once Shelly accepted Maggie and began helping her. The other girls seemed to be jealous. They would not accept Maggie into their group because of her 'living' in poverty. Being an 'A' student, didn't cut it with the snobs in Shelly's group.

"Shelly, are all your friends on the honor roll?"

"A couple of them are. The rest are just groupies. None of them understand what I am trying to do for Maggie. They want me to ignore her and get back with them. I don't feel a part of that group any longer since you introduced me to Jesus."

Loren smiled. She had seen the changes in Shelly and was pleased with the change. Now, they had a status problem. Somehow they needed to come up with a solution where all parties would be satisfied. Right now, all they could see to do was to pray for an answer. Loren led them into a short Bible study, then a prayer for guidance. Both girls left feeling somewhat better, but the problem was still unsolved. Kit called to them to say 'goodbye'. Both waved to him, then climbed into the car with Diane.

CHAPTER 11

Maggie was coming down the school steps at the close of school, when she saw a couple of Shelly's friends climb into a bright red convertible. With a second glance, she recognized the boy driving. Derek Mason! He was trouble! Maggie whirled around, her eyes searching the school grounds for signs of Shelly. She had to know about this! Quickly she walked back toward the student parking lot where Shelly would probably be waiting for a ride home. As she walked, she heard the screech of tires coming from the convertible making a big show of power and speed.

Shelly was just coming out of one of the side doors when she saw Maggie. Before she could wave a friendly greeting, Maggie came running up to her.

"Shelly! A couple of your friends got into Derek's car just now!"

Shelly's face turned white. She reached out and gripped

Maggie's shoulders.

"Who?"

"It looked like Bonnie and Jackie. Derek had another one of his buddies with him."

"Come on. I think I know where they will go."

Both girls caught one of their senior friends, Diane, who had a car. Breathlessly, Shelly told her why she needed a ride. The girl knew about Derek and quickly offered help, Everyone piled into the car and Diane quickly shifted into gear as she backed out of the parking space.

A couple corners were turned almost too sharply, but they were on their way.

Shelly remembered the time when she had first met Derek and had agreed to join him in a car ride. She didn't remember how she ever got out of that situation, but she had.

She glanced over at Maggie who was hanging onto the seat. Shelly handed over her purse to Maggie.

"Get my cell out and turn it on. We might have to call 9-1-1."

After driving at an unsafe speed, the girls spotted the red convertible far ahead of them getting ready to turn off the highway onto a dirt road. Diane slowed down, not wanting Derek to spot them. Derek was probably taking them to the old cabin where he usually took his 'dates' . Diane stopped the car at the turn-off.

"Okay, I know where they are going." She reached over to Maggie and retrieved the cell phone. "Let's pray, Maggie, then I will call for back-up."

Maggie nodded and stretched out her hand to take Shelly's as they prayed aloud. When Shelly was finished, she dialed 9-1-1. Slowly she explained what had happened and what would surely follow if they didn't get there soon.

"No sirens, please. That will scare them off. I'll wait at the turn-off so you will know where to go."

Shelly closed the cell and put it down. Now, the three girls waited.

Derek took Bonnie's hand and pulled her into the cabin. Jackie was ushered in by Derek's friend, Joe. "Come on, baby. This is the fun part. The climax of the ride."

He was holding tightly to Bonnie's shoulders standing close. She could feel his breath on her face. It almost smelled of alcohol. This was not what she wanted. She had ignored all the warnings from other girls who had been in this same situation. She heard Jackie shriek in the next room. How were they going to get out of this? How far from town were they? Bonnie turned her attention back to Derek. She felt his hands on her. He had begun to unfasten the buttons on her blouse. His hand was reaching inside…. She felt like a deer caught in a bright light on the highway. She felt defenseless. Oh, how she wished she had listened to Shelly! Her bra was unfastened and the bottom of the blouse pulled free of her skirt.

The front door banged open and two big policemen shouldered their way into the room. Derek jerked back pushing Bonnie back against the wall. She regained her balance and nervously began securing the buttons on her blouse.

"Up to your old tricks, Derek? Put your hands up."

"Officer, she came willingly. We aren't doing anything wrong."

"Maybe not yet, but this girl is underage."

The other policeman brought Joe out, holding him by the collar of his shirt. Jackie followed, then scooted over to stand beside Bonnie.

"Which one of you girls has a driver's license?"

"I do." said Jackie.

"Then you drive that convertible back to town. We're taking these fellas to jail."

He tossed her the keys after getting them out of Derek's pants pocket. They all turned then to go outside. Bonnie finished tucking her blouse in, then walked to the door. She looked at Jackie. They had learned their lesson the hard way. She was close to being raped and possibly beaten. How had the police known about this? Finding out really didn't matter now. They were safe and could hurry home, pretending this had never happened. Both were shaking in fear. Slowly they began to realize the danger they had been in and it would have been worse.

As Diane was driving Maggie and Shelly home, Shelly voiced her thoughts about their problem with the 'shunning'. They followed Derek's car back toward town along with the police car carrying Derek and Joe in the back seat.

"Somehow we will figure this out, Maggie. How do your friends feel about continuing with the Bible Study and learning about make-up and stuff?"

"I'm not sure about the Bible part, but they sure want to learn all the other. I'll talk to them and see where we can go from here. I appreciate the ride Diane."

Diane let Maggie off at her home, then drove Shelly around the block to her home and driveway. Shelly thanked Diane for the help. They couldn't have done it without her. Diane mumbled an answer and drove away. The excitement of the chase fresh in her thoughts. Never before had she done anything like that. Saving Bonnie and Jackie was really an act of bravery. How had Shelly known where Derek was taking the girls? Had she been in a similar situation?

She didn't know much about either of the girls, but she was glad she had been able to help out when they needed it. Maybe she should check in on that 'beauty treatment' Shelly mentioned along with the Bible study. She had attended church and hadn't found it too dull. Everyone was a lot older, more like everyone being her parent's ages. Yes, she would just ask Shelly about it the next day at school. The program just might make church a little more interesting if Shelly and Maggie could get their classmates into church.

At school the next day the event of yesterday was almost on everyone's lips. Several versions were floating about the halls. The boys who created the happening were back in school after being bailed out of jail by their parents. Shelly could see the fear on her two friend's faces who had been taken to the abandoned house. Lunchtime, all of Shelly's friends joined her in the lunchroom. They couldn't apologize enough to Shelly for the way they had treated her. When Shelly could get a word into the conversation, she told them it was Maggie who had seen Jackie and Bonnie get in the car with Derek and his buddy.   Both girls then mumbled their thanks to Maggie. Maggie gave them both a wide grin and told them she hoped there were no hard feelings.

They went their way and Shelly and Maggie returned to their meal. Time would tell about their plans with their Bible studies and another get-together at Loren's home.

***

Andy came running into the living room. He grabbed Loren around her waist, swinging her around a couple of times before setting her back down. Planting a smacking kiss on her lips, he stood back, still holding onto her by the shoulders.

"Guess what? Loren, I think we have done it. I have six boys at the Church wanting to play basketball . We can start practicing next week.   I talked to the school principal and the school will let us play our games in the gym on off nights of the varsity team games. For now, we can use the court at the Park."

"That is wonderful, Andy. Our prayers are being answered. Let's get a tall glass of iced tea to celebrate. I made some chocolate chip cookies and still have some if Kit hasn't eaten them all."

"Do you suppose some of your girls might like to be cheerleaders?"

"I'll ask when I see them again. They had some suspense yesterday with a couple bad boys." Loren continued telling Andy what had happened. The troublemakers would have to be kept under careful watch now that they knew who had turned them in to the law.

CHAPTER 12

The first basketball practice was held on the court behind the church at the City Park.   Almost all the teens were there. The girls were ecstatic about being asked to be the cheerleaders. They found a few old pompons in the girl's locker room at school and were waving them around near the bleachers . Some of the boys were feeling real important. They had their own cheerleaders. They hadn't made the school team, but here they were playing . Kit was trying his hand at playing, too. He was only nine, but could fill in. Andy blew the whistle. All the boys gathered around. One of the other fathers volunteered to be the referee. The cheerleaders shouted out a cheer, then waved their pompoms about. The game was on!

A couple of the boys showed great potential. Their grades had kept them off the varsity team at school. Here, they could play for the fun of just playing. Andy blew the whistle a couple of times stopping the game. Some of the boys wanted to 'hot dog' and be the shooter all the time. Several times they were not even close or in position to shoot the basket, so they missed. One of the other players was close, but no one threw him the ball.

Andy was pleased by the turnout and the way the boys played. With a few more practices, he would approach another school close by and see if they wanted to have a game with their second and third squad.

Even the second or third string from the varsity would work and build up confidence in his players.

All of the boys were tired. They were not in shape to play a full court game like the varsity boys did. Andy noticed how sluggish they were playing halfway through the game. He called time and ended the game. If they got too tired, they would get discouraged and quit. Andy packed up the balls with Kit's help. A couple of the girls policed the stands. They didn't want any official from the city to find fault with them being there. They were just excited about being chosen for the cheerleading positions.

Loren watched the boys visiting with the girls and was thinking about maybe possible trouble with the other teens. The lights were turned off and they climbed into their cars. Time would tell soon enough if all was well among the teens. Andy set up another practice and exercising time. The boys needed to get their bodies in shape if they expected to play on a full court. The one at the church only had one basket on a short concrete slab. Andy could have the boys practice on the half court at the church until they regained their stamina. Even though the games would be outside, they would have the advantage of overhead lights and hopefully good weather to play their games. A practice in the school gym would come later now that school was almost over for the year. A whole summer was stretched before them to use the school gym when the church court would not be available.

The church members proposed a party for the teens on a Saturday night after graduation the following week. Fancy invitations were made up and mailed. Everything was working out. Some of the parents attended church service the following Sunday morning to see what had gotten their 'kids' interested in attending church services. Even though they were not a regular church attendees, they appreciated what the church congregation was doing for their teen. As they listened to the minister, new hope surged through some of the people. Some remembered the Bible stories they had heard when they were young and had attended a local church. Why couldn't they attend church? It was only an hour on Sunday. It was not like they would be missing anything on TV or other events held at different times of the year. Surely they could give the church an hour on Sunday. So, the church attendance grew. Families came together and learned the Bible stories once more as adults.

Soon, some of the new adults were gently included in some

of the other church activities and functions. They now felt like they belonged. Even though some of their kids halfway was reluctant to come with them to church, they remembered what Andy and Loren had told them about that being part of their program.

Jeremy was walking across the lobby of the bank where he worked on his way back to his desk when he overheard the name 'Camden'. That was Loren's married name! His steps slowed as he sort of listened in on the three men talking there in the lobby. They were talking about Andy and some computer chip that he had invented. NASA! It would be used in space? Wow! This was big! Jeremy shifted the stack of papers in his arms to look busy and not draw attention to himself.

One of the men mentioned going out to the Camden farm and searching the workroom. Grayson Electronics was then mentioned as being where the chip was assembled. Jeremy set his papers down on a nearby desk where he could listen and work at the same time. One of the men saw him there, but didn't suspect Jeremy of listening in. He wouldn't know what or who they were talking about anyhow.

As Jeremy watched the men leave, a cold chill went down his spine. These men could be dangerous. Loren could be hurt. Should he warn her? The answer 'Yes' came up in his mind before he could even think of a way out. Maybe he should approach Mr. Grayson first. Jeremy stewed about it for another half hour as he tried to concentrate on his work. Glancing at his watch, he noted it was close enough to lunchtime to take off. Carefully he set the folders of his work into his right hand desk drawer for later. If he could beat the traffic, he could catch Mr. Grayson before he went to lunch.

Mr. Grayson had just gotten off the elevator when he spotted Jeremy coming toward him. He still didn't like the man after the way he had treated his daughter, Loren..

Jeremy approached Mr. Grayson and tried to smile.

"Sir, I need to talk to you. Join me for lunch?"

"All right, Jeremy."

As they entered the restaurant, the coolness of the interior surrounded them. The heat of the day made the inside feel good to the men. A table was available near the back and they both sat down. Jeremy began telling him about the three men in the bank and what they were talking about. Mr. Grayson looked worried. He hadn't considered the chip being dangerous enough for anyone wanting to steal it. Andy and Loren might need more protection than the one man Mr. Browning had sent them.

"Why are you telling me this, Jeremy?"

"I cared once for your daughter and I don't want to see her hurt. I don't know what those men would do, but at least you will know about it ahead of time. They looked dangerous."

"I appreciate your honesty and telling me this, Jeremy."

"I was going out to see Loren, but thought I had better see you first. The men mentioned your company. If they hadn't, then I would have gone to see Loren."

The two ate their lunch, then went their own ways.

Gray Grayson returned to his office and informed his secretary that he was not to be disturbed. He closed his door and went to sit at his desk. Taking the phone in his hand as he sat down, he dialed Loren's home. After three rings, Loren answered.

"Why hello, dad. How are you?"

"I'm fine. Is Andy home? May I talk to him?"

"Sure. Hold on. He's in the shop." Loren went back through the house to reach the door to the workshop. She stuck her head in and called to Andy. "Andy, dad is on the phone. He wants to talk to you."

Andy put down his small screwdriver and reached over to pick up the phone. Loren stayed there long enough to see the frown on Andy's face before she returned to the living room to hang up the phone in there. Something was happening.

About five minutes later, Andy came into the living room where Loren was sitting. She looked up at his approach seeing the look on his face, she patted the empty cushion on the couch next to her. Andy walked over and flopped down. Running one of his hands through his hair, he then leaned back against the couch. Loren waited. She knew something was wrong, but waited for him to talk.

"Loren, your friend Jeremy went to see your dad today and told him about overhearing some men talk in his bank. They knew about the computer chip. Jeremy felt that you might be in danger, so he went to see your dad. I need to stay at Grayson's Electronics to work on this. Somehow, it has gotten dangerous.

I can't risk you or Kit getting hurt. Let's get some empty boxes and you can help me box up my stuff I have been working on. We need to get it to your dad's company shop as soon as possible. I'm not going to be able to continue working here. I thought the danger was gone. Kurt had already gone back to his other job since I had moved everything to your dad's plant. Those men might think some of the chip is still here at the house and I am working on it here, too."

Together they worked carefully packing the units Andy would need to finish the computer chip. He drove the car around to the back of the shop and the two of them loaded everything in the trunk. Now, the shop just had miscellaneous parts. They locked up the house, then drove into the city. Kit was with friends and was told to stay there until they came for him.

Kit watched TV along with Jason and the other members of the family. He was restless. What was taking Loren and Andy so long? He got up from the couch and walked over to the front window. A strange car was parked over on the other side of the street. It was black and its occupants were still inside. The hairs on the back of his neck raised as he felt he was in danger. That car looked a lot like the one he had seen along the dirt road when he had ridden his pony following the jeep from their back yard that one day. Kit walked through the house to the back door and slipped outside. His friend and family were intent on the program on the TV to even notice that Kit had vanished out their back door. Before Kit did, though, he grabbed a pencil and piece of paper from beside the phone.

This time, he would write the license plate number and all the descriptions he could of the occupants inside. Bent over and moving quickly, Kit slipped through the shrubbery between the houses and hurried down the street toward the park. He didn't dare cross the street and risk being seen. When he was far enough away, he ventured across the street stopping behind a large tree near the entrance. Were the men looking for him? Why? They didn't know him. Were they some of the same men who had come out to his house to break in for the computer chip?

Kit crouched down on his knees then focused on the license plate. As he started to write, the car door opened and the driver stepped out. The man started up toward the house and a second man soon followed.

Kit scribbled down the license number, then wrote down descriptions of the men. He couldn't go back to the house now. If they were looking for him, he needed to leave the area. With his heart pounding and sweat starting to trickle down his forehead, he began to run farther into the park. Hopefully the men would not see him.. He patted his pockets. Yes! The cell phone was still there. Near the gazebo in the center of the park was the public telephone. Kit pulled out the cell and called Andy. After two rings, Andy picked up.

"Hello?"

"This is Kit. You need to come and get me. I'm in the City Park down the street from Jason's home. A couple of men in a black car are parked across the street from Jason's. They have already gone up to the house. I think they are looking for me."

"Okay. Hang tight. We will be right there. Call Chief Matthews and let him know the situation."

"All right.." Kit replaced the phone in his pocket, but left it on. He was curious about the men and what was going on at Jason's house.

Slowly he moved back toward the entrance of the park to see if he could see the car or the house from there. Standing behind the large oak tree, he looked down the street.   The black car was gone. Turning his back against the tree, he called the Chief.

Five minutes later, Andy drove up. Kit jumped into the back seat, closing the door behind him. He sighed in relief. Andy put the car in gear and drove farther down the street, then circled around to the other side of the park. Stopping the car, both of them turned around on the front seat and looked at Kit.

"What happened, Buddy?"

"I was watching TV and getting bored. I got up and went to the front window and saw the car. It looked like the same one that came to the farm. I got out the back door and ran. Can we call Jason and see if they are okay?"

"Sure." Andy called, letting the phone ring more than five times. It started to go into the voice mail. Andy hung up. He put the phone down and put the car into gear. Slowly they drove down the street to a place where they could look across yards and see Jason's house. The black car was gone. Should he chance going over there?

"Stay here. I'll be right back. Loren get behind the wheel just in case we have to make a run for it."

Andy began cutting through the yards to reach the other street. Slowly he looked around to make sure no one was there before he walked up the front walk. Knocking on the door, he waited. No one answered. Andy turned the doorknob, finding the door unlocked. He eased the door open. Signs of a struggle was evident by the upturned chairs and table lamp on the floor with glass scattered around it. Where were they? Had they been kidnapped and held captive?

Andy went out the front door, closing it behind him. Loren had driven around to the front of the house and was waiting with the engine running. She looked over at Andy for instructions as to what to do next.

"Police headquarters. They need to know what is going on."

"I called them, but they acted like I was calling in a prank."

"Well, we'll straighten this out. There was no one at home. There was a struggle. We need to get the family back. They have nothing to do with any of this."

At police headquarters, they all met with Chief Matthews. He remembered Kit's call, but took it as a prank like Kit thought. Now, he felt bad since he knew about the important computer chip and the dangers it was causing Andy.

The Chief put one of his best men onto the disappearance of Jason and his family. Andy drove on home. There was nothing more they could do. The answering machine was machine was blinking. Andy went to check the message. There, someone with a gruff voice told them about holding Jason's family and would exchange them for the computer chip. Andy went back into his workshop.

There, he had some spares that did not work. He picked one and made sure it would not work, then set it down on the kitchen counter.

"This might be good enough to get your friend's off the hook." He looked at his watch. In a little more than an hour, he was to bring the chip to the park, leave it near a certain tree and leave. The family would be returned to their home after the chip was picked up. Andy told Loren and Kit what was happening. They listened, then, they made a circle around the table holding the chip and prayed for guidance.

God had to be in control. Andy called the Chief and let him know what was happening. The car was a stolen and was found abandoned near the junk yard at the other side of town. Where was Jason and his family? Were they at the junk yard?

The exchange was done and everyone waited. The police watched the man pick up the bag containing the computer chip and return to his car. Jason and his family were exited from the car and left there in the park. As the car drove away, the police flipped on their sirens and chased them down, then arrested the men in the car. Jason's family walked home from the Park. They were full of questions and wanted answers. Andy called them later and told them what then needed to know, plus thanking them for watching over Kit. With the men in jail and the dummy chip returned to Andy, life seemed to go back to normal.

Andy let it leak out that he was finished with the chip and it was sent to the Space Station in Florida for testing. All his paperwork and drawings went with it; leaving him free from possible conflicts with 'enemy agents'.

God prevailed at keeping them safe for future happenings. Andy indulged into another project with his communications. Loren helped him assemble parts in her spare time. They came to an understanding that no more dangerous gadgets would be made, just useful ones for their communications.

A couple weeks went by as they continued with their 'normal' life. When Kit brought the mail up from the mailbox, a large white envelope was there. The return address was NASA. Kit picked up speed walking toward the house. Loren and Andy were sitting on the couch when Kit came into the house. He handed Andy the mail with the white envelope on top. Kit sat down and impatiently waited while Andy opened the envelope. A gold embossed card was enclosed. Andy cleared his throat as he prepared to read the invitation.

"Here is our vacation for the summer. This is to inform you that you and your family are cordially invited to attend the pre-launch of the computer chip ceremony. After a couple days of preparing the chip in the part that goes into the space shuttle, you will be present to watch the space launch. Airline tickets will follow along with the information you will need to attend the ceremonies. Please confirm your attendance. Signed head of space exploration. Wow! What do you think about that? We are going to Florida!"

Andy grabbed Loren's hands and they did a little dance around the coffee table. Kit watched, then joined in the celebration. Wow! What a trip! School would soon be out and the whole summer stretched out ahead of him.

CHAPTER 13

Plans for the summer were starting to come together. The boys continued coming to the church to practice basketball and run laps. Soon, they would be shape to keep up with other players from their school and the visiting schools wanting to play them.

Graduation Day was soon upon them. The church planned a party for all the seniors who were graduating. A popular local band was called in and a stage was built on the concrete basketball court. The girls spent their time blowing up balloons with the school colors. Women of the church baked pies, cakes, cookies while some of the men set up their grills to fix hamburgers and hot dogs. Other men moved some picnic tables around and other foot long tables for the food and people to eat. Now, with everything decorated, the people would soon show up in a couple of hours.

Shelly fussed in front of the mirror in her bedroom. She couldn't decide on what hair style to wear to the church Graduation

Party. Her mother had taken off from work so she could attend the party. The whole town seemed to be in a festive mood.   Loren and Andy had presented her with a fancy dress to wear for the party. Twirling about from the mirror to look at the dress on the bed, Shelly smiled. It was the perfect color for her. Sunlight shone through the window making the dress sparkle. Small sequins were dotted across the front bodice.   Their silver and gold colors flashed with the sunlight.

Even though Maggie was not a senior, Loren and Andy had given her a dress, too. Craning her neck, Shelly looked out the window over toward Maggie's house. Was she just as excited as she?

When Shelly and Maggie stepped into the doorway of the church fellowship hall, they looked upon a festive group. A group of the high school boys who had formed a rock band was on the stage getting ready to play music to dance by. Even though the church did not hold to dancing, the dances were chosen carefully.

Line and square dancing were offered for all ages. If the teens looked upon these dances as 'old fogies' then, they needed to stay and watch. One of the church members stood in front of the microphone and called to all the teens to come onto the dance floor. Several reluctantly did. Joe signaled for the music to start. Tapping off the rhythm with his left foot, he started calling off instructions. Slowly at first, the teens followed the steps. Once they seemed to be catching on, the music quickened. Wow! Other teens jumped up to join in on the fun. Where in the world did these old people come up with such great steps?

The floor was soon full of dancing teens. Each was grinning and dancing to the tunes. As the music slowed and finally stopped, a break was called. When they helped themselves to the refreshments, they would begin again with a snappy line dance tune.

Shelly laughed as her partner took her elbow and led her off the floor toward the huge punch bowl. Loren winked at her as she walked around the room talking to several church members present. With a small grin, she secretly glanced over at Andy.

They had done it! The teens were in church!

No longer did church hold that boring, stuffy title. With a slight change in the music played in the Sunday morning services, slowly the teens came to the church. The music choices that Kit had on his CD of Contemporary music were used along with the Traditional songs. After a couple services, the members suggested to use the Contemporary music in the Sunday evening service. Most of the older adults were not familiar with the new songs and sort of rejected them. Some threatened to leave the church until they learned those songs would be sung only on Sunday night when most of them did not attend anyhow. The pastor had tried all kinds of different sermons on different topics to increase the Sunday night and Wednesday night attendances. Only the faithful few attended all three services. There was a difference between the Faithful committed and church members. With summer coming, even the Sunday morning services would suffer. Summer was vacation time. Going to church every Sunday through the summer was not popular with the members.

Graduation Day was finally here! The silky gowns and square hats were on everyone in a big sea of seniors. Soon the teachers and dignitaries were on the platform ready to start the ceremony. All of the parents were soon through milling about and found their seats. Silence settled over the large gymnasium.

With all the speeches said, the seniors started the line to walk across the stage and get their diploma. Cheers and claps sounded over the room. This was the big day everyone was waiting for. Summer was coming the following week and they were ready!

Even though some had not found jobs or were ready to vacation with their parents, the school would soon be empty and quiet. Cleaning crews would come in and repaint walls, fix leaky facets and scrub and wax floors. A few of the senior boys had applied for work doing some of it that would apprentice them into a job later on.

Shelly's mother hugged Shelly in a tight hug. She was so proud of her daughter! The two of them hadn't sat down to talk over their plans for the summer months or the fall. Shelly knew they couldn't afford college, but she really didn't know what kind of a job she could apply for. She and Maggie had planned to check into counseling at a summer camp nearby. Loren had told them that Kit was planning to go to the Boy's Camp near the girl's camp. If they became homesick, they could call him. Andy teased them. Kit nodded in agreement. He would probably be the one who got homesick. There would be no pony or dog to keep him company or a cookie jar full of chocolate chip cookies.

School was out officially for the summer. Andy and Loren were busy working on plans to keep the teenagers busy and in church. Several weeks went by before they could get the teenage girls and boys together again for some planned activities. Everyone was busy with their parents and other friends traveling.

Shelly and Maggie were both at loose ends. Neither one could really go anywhere with both of them helping out at home with their mothers. Summer was boring. What could they do? Most of the other teens were off on fabulous vacations or off to camp.

For them, money talked. Shelly stood beside her mailbox and extracted several brochures. One caught her eye. A girls camp! Ripping it open, she scanned the page. They were looking for teenagers as camp counselors. Great! Quickly she walked over to Maggie's home. She climbed the two steps onto the porch, then rang the doorbell. A few seconds later, Maggie came to the door. Seeing the huge grin on Shelly's face got her excited, too. She came out on the porch and they went over to the porch swing and sat down.

Shelly handed her the brochure. Maggie carefully scanned the page. She had never been to camp. What was a counselor supposed to do?

"What does a counselor do, Shelly?"

"Well, first off, they have to know more than the girls who attend camp. We are older, so we would qualify as counselors. Look, I don't have anything to do until I decide what to do when school starts up again. I don't have a clue about a job. Here is our chance to teach younger kids things that we know already and keep them out of trouble.

We can either work the whole summer or just a couple months at a time. You told me one time that you wanted to work with children. Here's your chance for some experience to put on your resume. Let's call and find out when we can go in for an interview."

Both girls went into the house and to the phone hanging on the wall beside the kitchen door. Shelly called while Maggie held open the paper for her to read. After three rings, someone answered. Shelly answered the questions, then motioned for Maggie to write down a time and place. On that coming Friday they were to come to the camp and be interviewed. Shelly thanked him, then hung up.

"Yippee! I think we are in! No one else has answered their ad. Now, I'll go on home and you go check out your wardrobe to see if we need to go shopping. When our mothers come home, we will tell them we have a summer job, uh, maybe. Okay?"

Maggie nodded. She walked Shelly to the door and watched through the screen door as Shelly almost skipped down the walk to go home. Turning back into the living room, she dropped her head. She had no clothes suitable to wear. Yes, she had several pairs of shorts and tennis shoes, but none really nice enough to be seen in public as a counselor. She could still check over the clothes that she did have and sort out maybe enough to make it through a month. A trip to the thrift store was needed, Maybe Shelly could go with her. Right now, though, she would set out the clothes she had. She knew a bathing suit, flip-flops and several short outfits would probably be enough. A couple dresses would probably be a good idea, too.

Maggie dragged out her battered suitcase from her closet. Placing it upon her bed, she began putting her chosen items inside. Frowning, she noticed that the clothes barely made a dent in the suitcase. She went over to her desk and sat down. Getting a clean sheet of notebook paper and a pen, she began making a list of items she needed to get. Shelly called awhile later wanting to know if she wanted to head for a thrift store. Eagerly Maggie pulled out her coin purse and put it into her purse. Skipping down the stairs, she went outside to meet Shelly.

At the first Thrift shop they entered, it was like entering a gold mine. All the outfits that they would ever need were found on the shelves, and on sale!

Taking several outfits to the fitting rooms, they began to try them on and decide which ones would look the best. Several accessories were also found, then off to the next store.

After going through two thrift stores, they sat on a park bench and checked their list. Shelly frowned. They hadn't found any comfortable shoes. Across the street was a Salvation Army thrift store. Grabbing up their purchases, they crossed the street and entered the store. Going right back to the shoe section, they began checking out the many selections found there. Most of the shoes were well worn and not comfortable on their feet. A little disappointed, the girls left the store. Pooling their money together, they decided to try a discount shoe store nearby. Several styles were shown as on sale. Their feet were listed as a popular size so the supply was small and picked over. Maggie found a pair of pink sneakers that she liked and was comfortable on her feet. They were barely under the amount of money she had left. When Shelly made her selection, they both left the store pleased with themselves for their thrifty shopping skills. Once more they pooled what money they had left and decided to treat themselves to a soda to celebrate their good shopping day.

They decided to take all their bags home first, then go get their sodas. If they happened to meet any of their former classmates, they wouldn't get kidded about their shopping haunts by the names on the outside of the bags. The less who knew about their low income the better.

The soda shop was crowded. Shelly found an empty booth in the back corner and they gratefully slid into the seats.

A blonde headed waitress came over and took their order. Looking around, no one was really that familiar to them. Breathing a sigh of relief, they enjoyed the noise, the music being played as they waited for their sodas.

One of the other seniors who had driven the car to help them get a couple of classmates of Shelly out of trouble, slid into the booth beside Shelly. Diane's eyes were a little puffy and red from crying. She dabbed her eyes before she made eye contact with the two. Both girls waited.

Diane gulped as she wrestled with her emotions before speaking to her friends. She tried a lopsided smile. Her voice was shaky and full of emotion. Diane had been wrestling with her need to change and let God into her life. She had seen the changes in both Shelly and Maggie. She wanted what they had. For the last few weeks she had fought the feelings of the Holy Spirit softly urging her to become a Christian. Now, she was ready.

"Shelly, Maggie, I need to have whatever you have in your life now. I have seen the difference in your lives and know that I can be more at peace once I have whatever religion you have."

"Oh, no, Diane. What we have is not a religion. Jesus Christ is a person who we have given control of our lives. What we have with Him is a personal relationship. By admitting that we are sinners, we confessed our sins and asked Jesus to come into our hearts to live. We are still sinners, but we are saved by grace. It is a daily walk with Him after that. Do you want to accept Christ as your Savior?"

Diane nodded. A few tears escaped from her eyes and slipped down her cheeks. Shelly offered Diane her hand as she reached across the table to Maggie with her other hand. Shelly prayed a short prayer for guidance, then asked Diane to pray.

The waitress saw the girl's heads bent so she waited before taking their sodas over to them. The third girl hadn't ordered yet. Leaving the sodas beside the soda machine, she walked on to take someone else's order.

Diane felt the peace settle inside her as she ended the prayer asking for forgiveness. She almost felt like shouting, but this was definitely not the place to do it. Her eyes shone as she looked at her two 'new' friends. Both of them had tears threatening to travel down their cheeks. Oh, how happy they were! The waitress was looming closer now and questioned her approach. Maggie saw her first and motioned her to come over to their table.

"Diane, do you want to join us in a soda? It will be sort of a celebration for you."

"Sure. Chocolate, please." she said as the waitress came forward. She placed Shelly and Maggie's sodas down on the table, then turned to go fix a chocolate one for Diane.

At the table near them sat Jackie and Bonnie. They had heard part of the conversation Shelly and Maggie had with Diane. Ever since they had been rescued from Derek and his buddy, they too, had felt the pulling of God. Looking at each other, they slowly got up from their table and approached Shelly and Maggie. Standing next to the table, Bonnie waited for Jackie to speak first.

"Shelly and Maggie, we have been watching you since you both have helped us that time with Derek with Diane's help. You have changed your life and seem to experience a happier attitude toward life. Can you tell us what it is?"

Shelly and Maggie scooted over in the booth for them to sit down. Diane wiped back a couple of tears. She listened as Shelly presented the plan of salvation to Jackie and Bonnie. With only a couple of questions asked, the two girls agreed to accept Christ as their personal Savior. This time there was some shouting from the number five booth. Some of the other patrons knew the girls and that they attended church. A few of them figured it was all a passing fancy and would soon grow old and probably die. How wrong they were! These girls were now a child of a King!

Shelly had successfully completed her 'journey of faith'. Maggie was on her way to finding her own 'journey of faith' through her closest friends.

CHAPTER 14

Kit walked out to the mailbox to get the mail of the day. Rufus the dog, went along for company. An official looking envelope was in the box. Carefully Kit pulled all the mail from the box and hurried back to the house. This **had** to be their plane tickets to NASA in Florida! He handed the mail to Andy and stood nearby to hear all the details.

Loren came in from the kitchen to see what all the noise was about. Andy turned around to look over at her. Andy saw the excited look in Kit's eyes.

"Here is what we have been waiting on. Come on and sit down. We'll see what and when we need to do for our trip."

Once Loren and Kit were both seated, Andy opened the envelope. There were three plane tickets and official looking badges for them to wear. The ceremony was scheduled for the following week. They would really have to scramble to get ready.

Suitcases were loaded in the car to prepare for their trip to Florida. Kit was excited as he handed Andy his small suitcase. He had never been anywhere there had been a beach to walk on and an ocean to splash around in. He also couldn't wait to see all the space vehicles displayed that had been in space.

Andy slid behind the wheel Loren and Kit climbed into the

car. Ranger nickered from the corral. He wanted to go too. The next door neighbor would take care of the place while they were gone the next two weeks.

Andy's computer chip would soon be placed in the hands of the space exploration team at Cape Canaveral.

A special airplane was waiting for them at the airport to take them nonstop to their destination. Kit was all eyes. He really couldn't believe his good fortune at being Andy and Loren's foster child. He was only eight years old, going on nine and he had everything a boy his age could ever want in life.

The next couple of days was like a whirlwind with no time to themselves. Everywhere someone was wanting them to come to see them. Andy even was offered a job in their plant to continue building his 'space' chips. If he wanted to continue that kind of project, he could work at home or at Grayson Electronics like he had been. Both of them had already agreed to keep to simple projects not dangerous to the family.

Kit took lots of photos of everything to show his friends back home. As they watched the rocket take off, Kit was really impressed with the rocket as it slowly climbed into the sky off its launching pad. Big billows of smoke rose with the rocket, then faded away as the rocket picked up speed and streaked into the heavens.

After watching the rocket outside, they went inside where

people were sitting at their computer monitors. There, Kit watched them map the rocket on its journey into outer space.

Two days later, the Camden family visited other attractions in Florida, then after going to the beach, they planned their trip back home.

There was no ticker tape parade or fancy speeches, but their church friends met them at the airport and drove them home. Boy was Ranger and Rufus glad to see them! Even the pony expressed the welcome home with the other animals. As the days passed, all three we able to get back into their daily routine. Kit still planned to go to a camp for a couple of weeks with Jason.

Andy and Loren reconnected with their teens who were attending church. The church now had a youth director who had been working with the teens in their absence.

The sanctuary of the large church was full for the morning's service. The organ was playing the final hymn softly as the congregation stood in their pews. Loren gripped the back of the pew in front of her. She felt the Holy Spirit at work! Her mouth was dry and the feeling of anxiety was with her. As the second verse of the invitation song was started, she watched almost all of 'her girls' stand and walk forward. They had all heard the Gospel and were ready to accept Christ into their lives.

Loren's eyes were filling with tears. Andy laid one of his big hands on top of hers as they watched. Out of the corner of his eye, a couple of 'his boys' moved forward to join the girls at the altar. Their monthly efforts to prepare the teens for this journey of faith had finally rewarded them with blessings too numerous to count.

A big fat tear finally fell from Loren's eyes on top of their clasped hands. Yes, this journey was finished, but life's journey for the teens was only beginning.

EPILOGE:

FIVE YEARS LATER:

The birthday party was in full swing. Children all ages under 12 were milling about looking over their surroundings and waiting for the cake and ice cream. Zach could care less about all the noise going on in another room. Zach wiggled around on his stomach as he tried to get into the wing-backed chair in the sunroom.

This was a monumental task for a five year old. His one year old sister's birthday was today.   She was getting all the attention in the noisy other room .   No one really cared about him right now. He gave a small sigh of relief. He was now in the chair and wiggling around to sit up straight like an adult. Grandpa had told him that this was the very chair where his mom had sat during a big party she really hadn't cared about.

Grandpa had purchased the chair from his friend's home where the chair was originally. His five year imagination was geared to act as he tried to visualize how his mom had felt while sitting in this very chair. She had told him about the noisy music, then about the long dress she had worn.

Pretending he was her, he rubbed his back against the back of the chair. He pretended he was wearing the gown with the itchy material. Zach wiggled a little, scratching his back on the chair. Hadn't mom also said something about going outside in the garden?

She had, and one of the men she knew had come out to join her. Zach wrinkled up his nose. *Girls!* Yuck! Gramps had told him he was too young to worry about liking girls. Zack smiled as he leaned back in the chair. His dark brown eyes looked at the designs on the ceiling.

Someone had come up behind the chair as a shadow moved across the ceiling over him.

Zach smiled up at his mom.

"Hi Mom. Is the cake and ice cream ready yet?"

"Yep. What are you doing way out here in this old chair?"

"I was just thinking about you. I was trying to imagine how you tried to like the party all those years ago when you sat in this chair."

Loren laughed and took a hold of one of his hands pulling him out of the chair and onto the floor. "Come on. Let's party!"

Her thoughts went back to that day. It was the start of her life, really. The chain of events that followed had led her to this time with a family. The time had gone so fast. Here she was with a five and a now a one year old. Their foster child, Kit, was now a teenager. Life was good. Andy and her now had a full family. Her journey of faith had brought her to helping teens search out their 'journey of faith'. Hopefully those who had accepted Christ will want to reach out to their other friends with the message of salvation.

ABOUT THE AUTHOR

LAURA E. FEDERMEYER grew up in a small town in Ohio where she lived with her parents and two younger sisters. Laura had always loved to write and make up stories about cowboys and horses. As a teenager, she accepted Christ as her Personal Savior and began writing stories for church publications, contests, etc. Several of her writings were published and she won second place in a writing contest.

She moved to Florida in 1967. She met an older lady who had horses and cows. Laura was able to fulfill one of her dreams of being a 'cowboy.' Several years later, she was able to buy her own horse.

Her next dream was having a home in the country and that came true when she married Richard, her husband. Now, both are retired and enjoying the country life.

This will be Laura's third book. The first is *Loren's Journey of Faith*, second, *The Mystery of The Old Mill* and now this book, *Faith Continues its Journey*.